AGAINST THE LAW

OTHER FIVE STAR WESTERN TITLES BY RAY HOGAN:

Soldier in Buckskin (1996)
Legend of a Badman (1997)
Guns of Freedom (1999)
Stonebreaker's Ridge (2000)
The Red Eagle (2001)
Drifter's End (2002)
Valley of the Wandering River (2003)
Truth at Gunpoint (2004)
The Cuchillo Plains (2005)
Outlaw's Promise (2006)
Fire Valley (2007)
Panhandle Gunman (2008)
Range Feud (2009)
Land of Strangers (2010)
Desert Rider (2011)
Apache Basin (2012)

AGAINST THE LAW

A WESTERN DUO

RAY HOGAN

FIVE STAR

A part of Gale, Cengage Learning

Detroit • New York • San Francisco • New Haven, Conn • Waterville, Maine • London

GALE
CENGAGE Learning®

LIBRARY OF CONGRESS CATALOGING-IN-PUBLICATION DATA

Hogan, Ray, 1908–1998.
    [Novels. Selections]
    Against the law : a western duo / by Ray Hogan. — First edition.
        pages cm
    ISBN-13: 978-1-4328-2631-4 (hardcover)
    ISBN-10: 1-4328-2631-X (hardcover)
    I. Hogan, Ray, 1908–1998. One more hill to hell. II. Title.

813'.54—dc23   2012046355

First Edition. First Printing: April 2013.
Published in conjunction with Golden West Literary Agency.
Find us on Facebook– https://www.facebook.com/FiveStarCengage
Visit our website– http://www.gale.cengage.com/fivestar/
Contact Five Star™ Publishing at FiveStar@cengage.com

Printed in Mexico
1 2 3 4 5 6 7 17 16 15 14 13

ADDITIONAL COPYRIGHT INFORMATION

CONTENTS

7

★ ★ ★ ★ ★

ONE MORE HILL TO HELL

★ ★ ★ ★ ★

I

Dan Grimshaw sat quietly in his saddle, a high, square shape in the faint light. His lean face was set, a smooth gravity laying its stillness over his features while his eyes probed thoroughly the scattering of poor buildings of the run-down homestead. About him and all around him a spring dawn was flooding down from the hills to the east, spreading swiftly over the prairie, tinting the grass purple, and changing the land to a restless sea of color.

"Tough," he murmured. "Tough for a woman."

He shrugged then, something in him seeming to crystallize, forcing him to a decision.

"Miz Olmstead!" he called out.

The door of the small frame shack flung back at once and Melissa Olmstead stood in the opening. Lamplight was a yellow glow behind her and the morning's soft wind pressed its gentleness against her dress, molding it to her figure in sharp relief. The mass of dark hair that Grimshaw had noted before, when on occasion he had passed the place and seen her in the yard, was a glinting halo about the pale oval of her face.

She was thoroughly womanly, cut to move a man deeply, and Grimshaw was immediately aware of Caine Pomeroy's reasons for friendly overtures and his gloved treatment in evicting her from Kingpin range. His treatment of other homesteaders had been less tolerant—ruthless, brutal raids in the night, fire, gun play—and in the end they had all drifted on, broken and

11

defeated, unable to withstand Kingpin's merciless power and far-reaching influence.

All, that is, but Melissa Olmstead who, perhaps, after the death of her husband had less reason to stay than any. Alone she had remained, stubbornly refusing Pomeroy's offers, facing him as she faced Grimshaw now, bitter, defiant, and with an old carbine rifle held firmly in her hands.

"Well?" she said coolly.

" 'Morning," Grimshaw answered, touching his wide hat.

"If you've come with some message from Pomeroy, you can save your breath."

Grimshaw shifted in the saddle, the silence becoming thickly uncomfortable between them after that. In the shed behind the house a horse stamped and blew noisily and a flock of crows, settling in the lower, untended field, flung their harsh cries into the gathering day.

"Pomeroy don't know anything about this," Grimshaw said at last. "I'm here as a friend."

"Friend?" Melissa echoed. "You're Kingpin, aren't you?"

He shook his head. "That's neither here nor there now. Take my advice and clear out today. Go back to your people. Pomeroy's through waiting."

Melissa's eyes flicked him with surprised interest, but suspicion had its strong way with her.

"Is that your advice . . . or Pomeroy's?"

Again Grimshaw shrugged, biting down the impatience that plucked at his lips. "I'm telling you as a friend . . . get off Pomeroy's range. I'm through at Kingpin. I'm moving on."

"Drifter," she murmured half aloud. Then: "What's the matter? Got your fill of seeing honest men beaten, whipped, killed, and run off their own land?"

Bitterness welled and surged through her words as the wounds reopened and Grimshaw could see the brave defiance and determination momentarily crumple on her face.

"Go back to your people," he said then kindly, a softness in him deepening his words. "There's nothing ahead of you now but trouble if you stay."

Abruptly he touched his hat and, wheeling about, cut toward the shallow valley where a winding stand of willows marked the broken, irregular course of the Shannin.

Reaching the stream, he dismounted, ground-reined the buckskin horse, and, taking a small lard bucket from his saddlebags, dipped up a bit of the clear water. He started a small fire. Placing the bucket over it, he sat back, waiting for it to boil.

He heard then the steady drum of a running horse and a tight furrow crowded his brow as he wondered upon it. The sound died, and, the water, reaching its peak, he poured a hand-ful of coffee into the bucket, watched the liquid rise, and then set it off, stirring down the froth with a twig. After it had cooled a bit, he lifted it to his mouth and drank deeply of the steaming brew.

The day's full-blown heat had begun to lay across the prairie by the time he was again in the saddle, and he pulled his hat lower against the rising glare. For a time he followed the Shan-nin, catching what he could of its vagrant coolness and letting his mind run back over Melissa Olmstead's words. He hoped she would take his suggestion and leave her small land holdings to Pomeroy, but he could not find it in his mind to blame her if she did not. After all, he was a Kingpin rider and she had no understanding of his thoughts.

Near noon he cut away from the valley and climbed the short hills toward Kingpin's main headquarters, lying in the flat hol-low of the Crude country. He paused briefly on the last crest, letting his eyes drift over the vast, rolling domain of Caine Pomeroy and he had a short moment of understanding for this cattleman's problem—grass was gold in this arid land which, once broken by the plow, went to dry dust under the summer's driving sun—but he could find no final justification for Pomeroy even in that thought. Suddenly anxious to get a bad chore over, he spurred the buckskin into a gallop, rode a few minutes later into Kingpin's yard, and pulled up before the rack of the bunkhouse.

He sat for a moment in the saddle, a feeling of something amiss running through his long frame. When he dismounted, he was conscious of a small tension building itself along his nerves, turning him wary. But there was no outward change in him as he looped the reins over the rack bar and walked the short distance to the main house where Pomeroy lived. He strode across the porch that ran the full length of the building, pulled open the screen door, and stepped into the front room, used by Kingpin's owner as an office.

Pomeroy was there, sitting behind the table made to serve as a desk, a long cigar uptilted in his small mouth, the sly malevolence of power lying boldly across his dark face. Behind him stood Britt Whitcomb, Kingpin's foreman, beloved of no man or woman and with no redeeming qualities in his nature but an unbounded devotion to Pomeroy and Kingpin. Two other riders, Alvy Ryan and a man named Joe Siddons, lounged in opposite corners of the room. Little flags of danger were sounding their warnings to Grimshaw then. He nodded briefly in greeting.

"Little early for you to come in," Pomeroy observed dryly.

"I'm quitting," Grimshaw said. "Like to draw what money I have coming."

"Why, now, that's right interesting," Pomeroy ran on in his mocking voice. "Especially when Britt here tells me he overheard you giving the little nester widow a little advice early this morning. Good advice, too."

Grimshaw stood quietly. He felt then, rather than heard, the fifth man in the room, standing in the corner behind him. And he remembered suddenly the sound of the running horse he had heard when he was making coffee early in the day. That must have been Whitcomb.

"One thing that bothers me, though," Pomeroy said after a time. "What's your angle? You're no nester."

"Maybe," Grimshaw said in a voice as dry as winter grass, "I don't like to see people pushed around."

"Don't worry about that, friend," Pomeroy said then. "Nobody is going to push that young widow around. I'm simply clearing my range and inviting her to come here, say, as my housekeeper."

Grimshaw's answer was brief. "Touch that girl and I'll kill you."

Caine Pomeroy eyed the tall rider thoughtfully. "You would at that," he mumbled. "Too bad. I like your kind and I could use you here on the ranch. But until I get my other troubles cleared, I expect I'd better fire you, and keep you here as my guest. Then I'll decide what's for you." Abruptly Pomeroy's bland casualness dropped away. "Take him to the old bunkhouse and keep a guard on him. If he tries to break out, cut him down."

Grimshaw felt the hard muzzle of a gun jam into his back. Siddons and Ryan stepped forward and relieved him of his pistol.

"Let's go," Ryan said, and kicked back the door.

Grimshaw turned, hearing Whitcomb's voice make its complaint: "Caine, about that widow. Now, we don't want no woman around here."

"Who asked you?" Pomeroy snapped.

"Means nothing but trouble. Just trouble," the foreman continued. "Just trouble."

15

II

The old bunkhouse was a small, one-roomed affair, abandoned some years back for the new structure which stood close by. It was completely barren except for a wooden bench running across one end, and Grimshaw, entering, sat down and watched as Ryan pulled the door shut. He arose then and slammed up the window over the bench. Instantly Ryan was there, gun in hand.

"Hot in here," Grimshaw said, and sat back down.

"Now, you heard what Caine said," Ryan warned. "Any foolishness and you're a dead man. Just behave until tomorrow, and then likely he'll send you on your way."

"Why tomorrow?" Grimshaw asked.

"Because . . . ," Ryan began, and caught himself suddenly. "I'm telling you nothing," he snapped. "You'll find out in time."

He turned then and watched as Siddons came across the yard, bringing a plate of beans and meat and a tin cup of coffee. Gun still ready, he waited while the man set them on the bench, and Grimshaw, finding himself hungry, ate his fill. Afterward, he stretched out full length on the bench and slept, knowing that little, if anything, could be done until after dark. Awakening near sundown to the clang of the supper triangle, he arose, stretched the stiffness from his muscles, and checked the yard from the window.

Smoke was curling up from the kitchen stack into the fading light and the night's sharp chill was beginning to settle over the valley. Ryan had exchanged guard duty with Siddons who sat, back to the wall of the new bunkhouse, facing the door to Grimshaw's cell. A half dozen horses stood hipshot at the rack, and Grimshaw mentally observed: *Three missing.*

A few minutes later Ryan brought him his evening meal— meat, beans, and coffee again—and placed it on the bench under Siddons's watchful eyes.

"Leave the door open," Grimshaw said then, trying to judge the temper of the pair. "Hot in here. I'm not going anywhere with you standing there with that gun in your hand."

Ryan stared at him for a moment. "Seems cool enough to me," he said, but he left the door wide. "Get your grub." He nodded to Siddons. "I'll watch him."

Grimshaw finished the plate and strolled to the door, coffee in hand. He sipped it slowly, making it last, and, when it was gone, he asked conversationally: "Been with Pomeroy long?"

Ryan waited a moment. Then: "Year or so, I reckon."

"Big outfit. That what made you sign on?"

Ryan grunted. "One job's as good as another."

Grimshaw shook his head. "I won't buy that, Alvy. A man's got to live with himself, and, if he's working for an outfit like Kingpin, there's going to be a lot of things in his head that bother him. Things that could make him look down his own gun barrel to forget them."

"Nobody bucks Pomeroy," Ryan said. "He's the power in this country and nobody moves unless it's all right with him."

"Not good," Grimshaw said, watching the man closely.

"Gets what he wants just the same," Ryan insisted, his voice lifting a little.

"Maybe so, but there'll come a day when he'll push the wrong man and that will be the end of him. It always happens sooner or later, and it don't matter how big the big man is, he'll be just as dead."

"So?" Ryan said cautiously.

"You ever wonder what happens to the men who have been doing the dirty work for him? Their protection's gone then and there's no big man to throw his weight around and keep the rest of the little people from taking them apart. They aren't afraid then, Alvy, and they start remembering old scores that have to be settled."

"And what do they do then?" Britt Whitcomb's voice said from the darkness beyond Ryan. "What happens then, mister?"

The foreman moved in beside Ryan and set a coal-oil lamp on the ground next to him. "Here, you can light this if you need it," he said. "You're doing a lot of talking for a man on a tight rope," he said to Grimshaw. "Maybe you'd like to tell me a few things, too."

The edge on the man's tone rubbed into Grimshaw. Whitcomb had always irritated him and the mere sight of the slight, hatchet-faced man with his close-set eyes was enough to rankle him. A match flared in the darkness, and Ryan touched the lamp's wick, filling the narrow corridor between the two bunkhouses with yellow light.

"I could tell you a lot of things," Grimshaw said, "all of which wouldn't sound very pretty to you."

Whitcomb stepped in close. "You're long on talk, drifter, but short on everything else. I told Caine you were a four-flusher when he hired you. I can name a few more things right quick."

Grimshaw's driving blow came out of the semidarkness and, missing the point of the jaw, connected farther back, and Whitcomb slammed back against the bunkhouse wall. The wind went out of the man in a gust, his hat flew off and rolled drunkenly away, and his pistol, jarred from its scabbard, fell to the ground.

Ryan was on his feet instantly, gun drawn, but Grimshaw stood quietly, rubbing his knuckles. He watched the foreman rise slowly. The hatred in Whitcomb's eyes was fire itself and for a long moment he stared at Grimshaw while fury plucked and tugged at the corners of his thin lips. And then, saying nothing, he picked up his gun, retrieved his hat, and walked off into the gloom.

"Now that was a fool thing to do," Ryan said, settling back down. "You're good as dead."

Grimshaw smiled, moving back into the room. "Maybe," he said, and began to pace the small quarters restlessly. He could feel Ryan's eyes upon him, hard and suspicious, but he knew there was doubt in the man's mind, too, and it pleased him to have it that way. Ryan would do a little deep thinking in the next few hours.

"Going to be a long night," he observed then, and stretched out on the bench again.

He could hear Ryan's grumbling reply. The clatter of dish-washing chores came from the kitchen of the main house, and one of the ranch dogs set up a monotonous yapping that carried hollowly out into the prairie. Evening faded into darkness, starlight strengthened, and the many shadows laid their irregular shapes upon the land. A door slammed, and Siddons clumped across the hard pack. Grimshaw could hear the low murmur of voices. After a time one—Siddons or Ryan, he could not tell which—returned to the main house.

Minutes later Grimshaw heard the door bang again and the sounds of men mounting to leather, and then the steady pound of horses as they left the yard in a rush. Raising his head cautiously, he looked through the window. Two horses remained at the rack, his and one other.

"Ryan!" he called, keeping his voice level.

"Ryan's gone," Siddons said. "What you want?"

"Sure like a smoke," Grimshaw said. Desire for action was sweeping him, urgent and demanding and unyielding, for, understanding the devious ways of some men, he knew that Pomeroy would strike that night if Melissa Olmstead had not accepted his advice. A tremor of anger went through him and there was a moment while he cursed all men such as Caine Pomeroy. But his voice was controlled and even as he said: "Need a light. Mind if I come out and use your lamp?"

Siddons considered for a time. "Come ahead," he said finally.

"But no monkeyshines!"

Grimshaw strolled through the doorway, rolling a cigarette. Stopping momentarily, he breathed deeply of the night's coolness, taking a quick re-check of the horses as he paused. Satisfied, he moved on.

"Get your light and get back inside," Siddons ordered irritably.

Grimshaw bent for the lamp. Tipping it sidewise, he caught up the funnel of heat from the chimney and the cigarette glowed into life. Drawing in a deep lungful, he exhaled smoke slowly, and then in a single movement flung the lamp straight at Siddons and lunged away.

Siddons's gun exploded into the silence and Grimshaw felt the searing burn of the bullet as it drove through the fleshy part of his thigh and spun him half around. It sent him off balance momentarily, but he crashed full weight into Siddons and they went down, rolling in the spreading flames. Grimshaw clawed at the gun and wrenched it away, and, as they swayed to their feet, struggling for its possession, he brought up his knee hard into Siddons's belly, and the man gasped and buckled. Grimshaw drove him to the ground with a blow to the ear.

Siddons came up unsteadily, and again Grimshaw dropped him with a hard fist. The man stiffened and lay still.

Sucking for breath, Grimshaw dragged him beyond reach of the fire and beat out the smoldering places on their clothing. Feeling then the sharp lance of pain in his leg, he wasted a minute while he bound the wound with his handkerchief, and then, half running, half walking, he reached the buckskin and swung up into the saddle and turned the horse about. Looking back once, he could see the fire spreading and caught a glimpse of the Chinese cook, peering out of a window in complete fright. Then he put the horse out of the yard and into the short hills at a dead gallop.

He saw the yellow-red glow hanging in the sky long before he topped the last rise and knew at once that he had been right in his calculations. The Olmstead place was burning, and he had his moment of hope that Melissa was not there, that she was gone, on her way back to wherever she had come from. But he felt no assurance and he knew the fact was something that must be settled in his own mind.

He had cut himself into this deal primarily because of a desire to see the right thing done, but somewhere it had stopped being a matter of objective consideration. He thought of the girl, as he had last seen her, and he remembered Caine Pomeroy's words and a coldness settled over him, turning him still, wiping the excitement from him and replacing it with a suppressed sort of fury. He swung away from the crest of the rise then, running the buckskin slowly until he crossed the dully sparkling water of the Shannin. He resumed the fast pace then along the spongy banks until at last he came to the point where he was nearest and just below the Olmstead place.

The house was a tower of crackling flames. The barn was a smoking ruin, but two or three small outbuildings yet stood, small blocks of darkness against the fire's color. Remaining in the concealment of the willows, Grimshaw could see Pomeroy and the rest of Kingpin milling about in the brilliantly lit yard, but there was no sign of the girl, and hope once again lifted within him. He recognized then the necessity for getting closer if he was to be certain, and, bending low over the buckskin's neck, he worked his way along the shallow draw that footed the homestead, to a point where it curved in closest and then moved swiftly in.

Luck was with him and he checked the horse at an out-size juniper and swung stiffly from the saddle. His bad leg gave away, and he clung to the saddle for a moment while the pain raced through him, and then slowly ebbed. Afterward, he

21

secured the horse and, favoring the injured thigh, moved in a dozen more yards to another growth of juniper.

This reached, he discovered that he still could not see or hear distinctly Pomeroy and his riders and, dropping flat on his belly, wormed his way toward a small tool shed standing somewhat to the side of the main house. Every movement in that prone position sent ragged flashes of pain through his leg and a wetness there told him that it had begun to bleed anew, but he crawled doggedly on until at last he was in the shadow of the building, with the bulk of the structure between him and Pomeroy.

He lay quietly for a long minute, letting the pain subside. When he was once again ready to move, he lifted his head and saw the girl crouching in the shed's protection. Gathering his strength, he got to his feet and lunged the short distance to her side. She whirled at the sound and her hand flew to her mouth in a gesture of fear.

"Don't make a sound," Grimshaw whispered. "You all right?"

Melissa looked at him for a full, breathless moment, the fear and surprise still dulling her senses, and then all at once she gave way and was in his arms, sobbing out her terror. All the cool reserve was gone, all the fierce pride—and she was as any woman in a man's strong arms, feeling their protection.

"You all right?" Grimshaw asked again after the storm had passed.

The girl nodded. "It was terrible. They came and Pomeroy asked me to come outside so we could talk. I did, and then they set fire to the place. One of them held me, but I broke away and hid, and they've been hunting for me. I lay in the ditch and one of them passed me by so close I could almost touch him. I was trying to reach the river, where I could hide in the willows."

She stopped after the rush of words and flung a long glance at the flames. "Everything I own in the world is in there," she said.

Grimshaw turned to look. His leg buckled and a spasm of pain ran across his face.

"You're hurt," she said quickly, but he brushed her aside, his eyes on Caine Pomeroy and his riders, still moving about the yard of the burning house. A man galloped into the fan of light, and Grimshaw recognized Siddons as the latter pulled up alongside Pomeroy and spoke rapidly. Kingpin's owner sat perfectly still until Siddons was through, eyes fastened to the backs of his hands folded on the saddle horn. Then he raised his head.

"Find that girl!" he ordered, his voice carrying plainly. "When we get her, Grimshaw will come looking for us."

Grimshaw turned back to Melissa. "My horse is tied to that big juniper down near the draw," he said, reaching into his shirt pocket. "Get on him and double back to the willows and follow the river until you're away from here. Ride to town as fast as you can."

"Nobody will help . . . not against Pomeroy," she said.

Grimshaw shook his head. "I know. Here's some money. There's a train that goes through about daylight. Buy yourself a ticket and go home to your people."

He pressed the money into her hand, and for a time she was still. Kingpin's men were moving about more widely now, yelling back and forth, extending their circle of search.

"And you?" she said finally.

Grimshaw shook his head. "I'll be all right. The big thing is for you to get out of here as fast as possible."

Again Melissa seemed to consider, and Grimshaw, impatient at the delay, pressed her to movement. "Not much time. They'll comb this place to the inch. You'll have to hurry and, if anything happens . . . don't stop. Keep going."

She said then: "Good bye, Dan. I wish. . . ."

There was a brief time when he felt her lips brush his own,

and then she was gone, running toward the juniper.

Watching Kingpin narrowly, Grimshaw checked the gun he had taken from Siddons and, finding it the same caliber as his own, replaced the spent cartridge in the cylinder. Glancing back once, he saw Melissa had reached the buckskin and was climbing into the saddle.

At the same moment a shout went up from one of the riders. Grimshaw turned to see the girl racing for the willows, and, bringing his gun up quickly, he laid a shot at the feet of Pomeroy's horse, checking the pursuit before it could get started.

"Don't move!" he called out.

A man swore and the plunging horses settled down after the echoes of the shot had drifted away. Dust and smoke lifted up into the night and Pomeroy's sardonic voice reached out and placed its aggravation on Grimshaw's nerves.

"Glad you're here. Saves us looking you up later, friend. Got a little matter to settle with you."

He stopped, apparently thinking Grimshaw would answer, but when an answer failed to come, he said: "Just sit easy, boys. The fire is dying down fast, and, when it does, there won't be much light. Plenty of time."

Grimshaw counted seven riders in view. One was missing, and he wondered if the man were elsewhere in the shadows, or just hidden by the last standing wall of the razed house. Cautiously then, keeping from sight of the men, he moved to the opposite side of the shed. The missing man was not in the yard, and Grimshaw realized that he was somewhere in the darkness, possibly circling around to get behind him or flank him while his attention was drawn to Pomeroy and the others.

The cold coolness was upon Grimshaw then, but this time he was also touched with a running excitement. His back to the shed, he replaced the cartridge he had recently fired and waited, listening for the slightest sound, the scrape of a man's clothing, the click of a boot as it clashed with stone. It didn't come, and in the rigid stillness his leg began to throb more intensely. The men on their horses, pinned down, squirmed in their saddles. The fire had dropped to a dozen small tongues flickering palely in the night, and back in the hills beyond the Shannin a coyote set up his complaint.

Tension built up until it was a great, oppressive thing, smothering the small clearing. Suddenly the last of the flames were out and there was only the star shine to break the dark solidness. Pomeroy and the others became indistinct shapes, vague shadows in the gloom. It was then he heard the man behind him.

Favoring his leg, he crouched and moved around the shed, reasoning that if he could no longer see Pomeroy and his men, they could not see him, either. Keeping low, he crossed the short space between the shed and the ruined house and pressed himself against the still warm wall. Horses were moving about quietly and the creak of leather and muffled *tunk-tunk* of hoofs in the deep dust were the only sounds.

"Get off your horses . . ."—Pomeroy's voice broke out of the darkness—"he can't get far."

"We'll get him, Caine," Whitcomb's voice came from across the yard. "Don't worry."

Grimshaw, standing silently against the wall, heard the distinct scuff of boots near the tool shed and waited in the blackness for the man to appear, to cross over and come to him. He held his gun waist high and ready, but the man, finding no one at the shed, called out—"Not here!"—and moved out into the open. It was Ryan, and he passed within twenty feet of Grimshaw.

Grimshaw started to go back, working slowly, hearing the sounds of the others beating around the yard and the other buildings. A horse stumbled and a man cursed, and another voice said irritably: "Get that horse away from here." Grimshaw moved on stiffly, picking each step carefully, keeping close to the building but far enough away to prevent the scrape of his clothing against the charred wood. He was rapidly becoming the center of the circling men and he recognized the urgency of getting away from the building, off to one side, if possible.

He felt the corner of the structure and waited, warned by some inner instinct, before making the turn. For several long minutes he was motionless, flattened against the smoking timbers, and then quite suddenly Caine Pomeroy, coming from the opposite direction, was before him.

Sheer animal hatred tore at the man's face and his gun blossomed bright orange in his hand, but Grimshaw was already lurching to one side. He felt the breath of the bullet even as his own gun added its flat, quick echo. Pomeroy fell backward from the shock of the heavy slug, and sprawled half in, half out of the burned house.

"Here! Over here!" a man shouted.

Grimshaw, on his knees, crawled for the protection of the tool shed, ignoring the pain that screamed through his leg. Feet pounded across the yard, slowed, and men came up to the prostrate figure cautiously.

"It's Pomeroy!" a voice said, peculiar in its high, wondering pitch. "He's dead!"

"Dead?" The answer was an echo, unbelieving. The impossible had happened.

Silence ran on for a time, nobody saying anything, each man having his own thoughts.

"I'm blowing this country," Ryan's voice said then, and Grimshaw smiled, thinking of the seed he had planted. A man's mind was a funny thing. An acorn of doubt placed there flowers quickly into a full-blown tree.

Ryan turned to catch his horse. The others watched, and

then they, too, were moving to their mounts and pounding out of the yard in a steady drum of hoofs. Only one man remained— Britt Whitcomb. He stood over Pomeroy's body and Grimshaw watched as he awkwardly removed his hat. His voice was choked, almost like a sobbing child.

"Don't you worry none, Caine. I'll square this for you. I'll take care of it."

Grimshaw knew then there was no future in that moment and, not being a man given to avoiding the consequences he had built up after the cards had fallen, he stepped out into the starlight. His own gun was in its holster as was Whitcomb's.

"Right here, Whitcomb," he said.

The foreman wrenched at his gun, fired briefly. Once again Grimshaw felt the wind of the lead and it threw his own aim wild. His bullet chunked into the wall behind the foreman. He fired the second time as Whitcomb brought his gun down from recoil. The man dropped, falling across Caine Pomeroy's legs.

Grimshaw staggered to the shed and leaned wearily against it. For a minute he was sick and the sharp odor of gunpowder was a mockery in his nostrils. Later, tired almost to insensibility by the strain and weakened by his own throbbing wound, he caught up one of the two horses, and, pulling himself into the saddle, started the long ride to town. The first rose streaks of dawn were just beginning to fan out from behind the eastern hills, and, as he topped the first rise, the lonely whistle of a train drifted through the quiet.

He pulled the horse to a stop, his thoughts having their strong way with him. That would be the train carrying Melissa away, taking her out of his life, taking her back to her home and people. The futility of his own life was heavy upon him then, and he felt worn and drawn and filled with a disgust for the uselessness of his ways. This could have been the country, the land, the valley, and she, he knew then, was the girl if only they

27

both had recognized it. Now there was only the next hill and the one beyond and the one beyond that until one day there were no more and a man was through with his riding.

He looked up, hearing the approach of a running horse. Quickly alert, he shifted his gun to a more convenient position and waited, following the sound as it came up the river. A horse and rider broke into view in the half light, and then Melissa was racing across the short distance toward him. Grimshaw swung stiffly from the saddle, leaning heavily against his horse, and, as she came to him, her face a mirror of her feelings, he took her into his arms.

"I couldn't go, Dan," she said. "I had to come back."

Grimshaw held her close to him, letting the pure song of it pour through his aching body, savoring every moment of it. He said then soberly: "You shouldn't have. I haven't anything to offer you except a long trail. I'm no sodbuster."

Melissa looked up at his face, eyes shining and bright. "Then we'll just ride on . . . but maybe someday we'll find the right place and stop."

★ ★ ★ ★ ★

AGAINST THE LAW

★ ★ ★ ★ ★

I

It sounded like a woman's scream.

Marshal Mark Kennicott, in the saddle since daybreak, came up with a jolt. He hauled the buckskin to an abrupt halt, listening intently, uncertain as to the source of the sound. For a time he remained that way, poised, rigid, his broad shoulders lifted, his wind-scoured face alert.

He relaxed and settled back. He guessed he was imagining things. It could have been a woman's voice, of course, but most likely it was just the cry of a cougar. The big cats sometimes screamed in almost human tones. And he had been only half awake. He had left Bakersville with the rising sun and it was now almost noon. But he was near home. Familiar landmarks told him Cameo Crossing was no more than two miles or so distant. He touched the buckskin with his blunt spurs and the tough little horse moved out at a fast trot. Be good to get back after a week's absence even though he knew the committee had something on its mind and would be waiting to see him.

The cry came again.

This time there was no doubt as to its origin. It was a woman's high-pitched, terrified scream. Coming from off to his left, from the direction of the widow Heaston's place he realized in the next instant. He wheeled his horse sharply off the trail and struck out across the rough, open ground toward a low ridge. On the far side of that lay the Heaston Ranch, or rather what remained of it; once a fairly nice little spread, it was now a run-down shambles since Will Heaston, who had been his friend, had died and left it to his wife Callie and their three daughters.

Callie and her girls had been a constant, plaguing worry since the day of the funeral. With no man around, Callie, Alberta, who was just eighteen, and the twelve-year-old twins were in continual danger from drifters and owlhoots who prowled the country. Several times he had attempted to persuade Will Heaston's widow to take her brood and return to their original home in Ohio but the somewhat large, attractive woman, despite her absolute inability to cope with the raw frontier life and manage the ranch her husband had willed her, insisted upon staying.

Once before there had been trouble. Two men on the dodge from Kansas law authorities had happened onto the isolated place. Their original plan apparently had included no more than robbery, but after observing the ranch for a spell and discovering it inhabited by two women and two small children only, they decided to move in and stay. It was by sheer chance that Kennicott, coming in response to a supper invitation, rode up and drove the intruders into the hills.

The buckskin pounded up the slope and topped out the rise. Kennicott's probing gray eyes at once picked up two figures in the hard-packed yard behind the weather-beaten house—Callie Heaston struggling with a squat, dark man. He was half dragging, half propelling her toward the barn that stood fifty yards or so to the rear. Kennicott could not see the back porch of the house where, undoubtedly, the girls were. At that moment Callie Heaston wrenched free of the hand clamped over her lips and screamed again.

An oath ripped from Kennicott. Hell of a note when a woman wasn't safe in her own house any more! One of the penalties of living near a cattle trail. Sooner or later every tramp in the West passed by your doorstep. And there was talk of forcing him to open up his town again. He drove the spurs home and started down the slope.

He reached the bottom and thundered across a fallow field— a field once plowed by Will Heaston for a corn crop but now turned to loose dust by the dry, relentless sun—and raced for the yard. The drumming of the buckskin's hoofs brought the man and the struggling woman to a stop. The drifter threw a quick glance over his shoulder, his whiskered face dark and belligerent.

Kennicott recognized him: Pete Sprewl, a troublemaker, a brawler who had run afoul of the law many times. That meant there was another man somewhere around—Sprewl's baby-faced brother Curly Dan, reputed to be somewhat of a gunfighter. Where you found one, you found the other. Kennicott had run them out of Cameo Crossing once before and he was unaware they were even in the territory. Apparently they had swung around Cameo this trip.

"Mark!" Callie cried, wrenching free as he came into the yard and pulled the buckskin to a sliding halt.

Her desperate cry sent anger flooding through him again. He left the saddle in a long dive, ignoring his authority, his gun, or the second man somewhere on the place. He struck Pete Sprewl shoulder on and they went down in an explosion of dust. Kennicott rolled to his feet and spun, driving his balled fist into the other man's broad face. He felt his knuckles smash into flesh and bone, heard the sharp, dry crack of the impact, and watched Sprewl go over backward.

Callie Heaston's fearful, anxious cries for her daughters were like a pointed goad digging into him. He lunged forward at the rising Sprewl and smashed him down again. Sprewl, lashing out blindly, grabbed Kennicott's leg and yanked. The lawman went down, breath gushing from his lips when he struck flat. Quick as a gun flash Sprewl was upon him, swinging with both ham-like fists.

Kennicott, on his back and at the mercy of those punishing blows, managed to twist sideways. He caught one of the drifter's arms and held on, turning hard. Sprewl's shape shifted to one side and the pressing weight of the man lessened. Kennicott jerked on the arm and in that same instant heaved upward with all his flagging strength. Sprewl's form toppled off to one side and Kennicott crawled free.

Across the back yard he became aware of the screen door's loud bang. And then the rapid tattoo of boot heels rapping across the hard pack.

"Mark! Watch out!" Callie's voice reached him.

He pivoted away, catching sight of Curly Dan rushing in to aid his fallen brother who remained sitting on the ground, rubbing his wrenched arm. Sucking hard for breath, the marshal braced himself for the attack from the younger Sprewl, weaving through the boiling dust toward him, head ducked low, knotted fists poised. Kennicott was tired. The exchange with Pete Sprewl had left him winded and his arms were heavy. He side-stepped as Curly Dan rushed in, stalling the younger man with two blows to the head. But he was slow stepping away and Curly Dan nailed him solidly with a right to the heart that rocked him.

Curly Dan's face was a hard, bleak mask. His expression did not change when he gritted out: "You've had this comin' from the last time, Marshal!"

Kennicott made no reply, only waited. He was going to let Curly Dan carry the fight to him, let the younger man do the moving in. He grinned his invitation and Curly Dan lunged for him. Again Kennicott glided away, landing a sharp blow on Sprewl's ear as he passed. Instantly Curly Dan spun, hoping to catch Kennicott off guard, but the marshal, veteran of many such moments, expected it and was waiting. When Curly Dan rushed in, guard down, he caught him flush on the chin. The drifter's head snapped back, his eyes rolled to the top of his head. He sank soundlessly into a heap.

From the tail of his vision Kennicott saw Pete Sprewl coming to his feet. He was dragging at the gun at his side. His back half turned, Kennicott dipped and spun away, drawing his own weapon. He fired in the same instant as the drifter. Sprewl staggered and clutched at his breast. For a moment he stared at Kennicott, a sort of vague wonderment in his eyes, and then he pitched forward and lay still.

Kennicott swung to face Curly Dan. The younger Sprewl was sitting up. He was looking at his dead brother, the same emptiness in his gaze. Slowly he got to his feet and swiveled his attention to Kennicott.

"You've killed him, Marshal. My own brother. Maybe it was a fair fight, I wouldn't be knowin'. But it don't matter. Point is, I'm bound to square up for him. And I'll be doin' just that." He turned away and started for his horse, tethered at the pole corral.

"Hold it!" Kennicott rapped sharply. "You're not leaving here just yet!" Without swinging his glance from the drifter he called out: "Callie? Everything all right up there?"

"All right," Callie Heaston replied. "You got here just in time."

"We was only hunting for a little somethin' to eat," Curly Dan said. "We wasn't hurtin' nobody."

"Sure, sure," Kennicott replied. "Your brother Pete had that in mind, I reckon. Good thing I got here when I did. If you'd hurt any of these women, a posse would have run you down and had you strung up before dark. I ought to run you in for just thinking about it, but like as not the reason for you being in jail would leak out and they'd have you swinging from a limb anyway."

Which, Kennicott knew, wasn't exactly the truth. Cameo Crossing residents, as a whole, thought little of Callie Heaston. Not knowing or understanding her problems, they had drawn their own conclusions as to her respectability living as she did, alone, beyond the edge of town. And the same applied to her eldest daughter.

"Now, get out of here," Kennicott added. "Get on your horse and keep riding. I see you around here again, I won't wait to ask any questions."

Curly Dan looked at him sullenly. His eyes shifted to the still form of his brother and back, questioningly, to Kennicott.

"I'll take care of him. He'll get a grave in town. Better than you'd dig for him out here in the hills."

Curly Dan nodded and moved toward his horse. He mounted up, in that leisurely fashion of his, and started across the yard. Halfway he paused. To Kennicott, he said—"We'll meet up again, Marshal."—and then rode out.

Callie and the twins were standing on the narrow back porch of the house when he reached it. Heaston's widow had an arm around each of her younger daughters who, now the danger and excitement were over, were chattering about the experience. Callie's face was flushed, still, and her blonde hair was awry. There was a red streak on one cheek where she had been struck and the sleeve of her dress was ripped half away at the shoulder. Her gaze was apologetic, and, when she met his grim look, she quietly began to sob.

The lawman moved up to her and placed his hands upon her shoulders. He shook her gently, softening a little. "It's all right now, Callie. It's all over with."

"I know, I know," she cried, releasing the two girls and throwing herself against him. She shuddered. "Oh, Mark! If you hadn't come when you did. . . ."

"Don't think about it," he murmured. "I did come along and

that's all that counts."

"I don't know how to thank you," she said then, dabbing at her eyes. "Seems I'm always beholden to you for one thing or another."

"Will Heaston was my friend, same as you are," Kennicott said. "No need for thanks." He paused, looking at her more closely. "The thing that worries me is someday I might not come along just in time. Then what?"

"I know what you're leading up to," she broke in with a shake of her head. "And it's no use. I can't move. First thing is I've no place to take the girls. Where could we go? And second, there's no money . . . only the thirty dollars a month I get from Father's estate and that barely feeds us and buys the things we have to have. This house is paid for, otherwise we couldn't make it at all."

"Then, if you will live here, you've got to hire a man to work. No matter whether you need him or not for that, you've got to have one around. Just having him on the place in sight will keep the drifters from stopping."

"You know the answer to that," Callie said tiredly, brushing at her hair with the back of a hand. Despite her size she was well-proportioned and with proper clothing and a bit of make-up she would be more than attractive. "A hired man has to be paid."

"If you'd just let me help a bit . . . ," Kennicott began, but she cut off his words. He had offered before, even tried trickery maintaining he had owed Will Heaston some money but she had not been fooled. And the answer was always the same.

"Charity. I want none of it, Mark. I know you mean well. But I'll take charity from nobody."

The twins had turned away and were heading for the house. Kennicott watched them go thoughtfully. Suddenly he realized something. "Where's Alberta?"

Callie Heaston looked out over the littered yard, toward the low hills beyond the decaying barn. "I wondered when you were going to ask. She's working."

"Working? Where?"

"Jergenson's Café. As a waitress. She started this morning."

Kennicott stared at the woman for a long moment, with strong disbelief, and sighed. "You shouldn't have let her do that, Callie. You know what a lot of the town thinks."

Callie nodded. "Yes, I know what they think. Of her and of me. But you know it's not true. And Alberta's no child any longer. She impressed that upon me when I tried to talk her out of it. And I can understand the way she feels. She's just plain sick and tired of being poor, of being nobody. The five dollars a week Jergenson will pay her will be a small fortune to her."

Kennicott shook his head. "There will be a lot more than five dollars' worth of heartaches for her. I'm sorry she took the job. It means nothing but trouble."

Callie moved her shoulders in a helpless gesture. "You can't hold an arm over your children forever. They grow up."

Kennicott frowned. "Grow up?" Then he, too, shrugged. "I guess I hadn't realized."

Callie Heaston smiled. She glanced toward the house. "Near dinner time. Won't you come in and have a bite to eat?"

"Thanks, no, I've got to get on into town. There's a little unfinished business waiting for me." He noticed the woman looking over her shoulder at the body of Pete Sprewl, lying in the yard. The tautness of her face betrayed her horror at suddenly noticing the drifter again. "I'll take care of that," Kennicott said. "Thanks again for the invitation to eat. I'll take you up on it one of these days soon. *Adiós.*"

"Good bye," Callie murmured.

Kennicott swung on his heel and crossed the yard to where Sprewl's horse waited. He led the animal back and, after shouldering the drifter's body across the saddle, tied it down securely. Mounting his own buckskin, he took up the horse's reins and started for the trail. When he left the yard, Callie Heaston was not in sight. Death was one of the things she could not bring herself to accept.

But Mark Kennicott was not thinking of Callie Heaston. He was thinking of her daughter Alberta, and the problem she now would present.

And he was thinking about the committee of Cameo Crossing businessmen who were awaiting him.

II

Kennicott rode straight down the center of Cameo Crossing's main street, trailing the horse with Pete Sprewl's body draped over the saddle behind him.

He nodded to a few acquaintances who fell into the procession. By the time he had traveled the distance between the high, false-fronted buildings of the town to the office of Doc Cartwright, the coroner, he had accumulated a fair-size crowd. Two of which, he noticed, were members of the citizen's committee. Jim Dry, who owned the feed and hardware store, and Paris Humboldt, the banker. He stepped from the buckskin and faced Cartwright, a thin little man in a dusty suit that was well stained with chemicals.

"Who's this, Mark?"

"Name's Pete Sprewl. Tried to gun me but I was a little luckier than him."

"Stranger to me," Cartwright said, taking the dead man's chin between his fingers and twisting the face around to where he could better see it. "Well, a couple of you boys untie him and tote him inside. Any special details about it, Marshal?"

"He and his brother were giving the widow Heaston some trouble. I just happened by. You need a statement of what happened from a witness, we'll ride out and she can give it to you."

Cartwright favored the lawman with an enigmatic glance. "The widow Heaston, eh?"

There was a breakup in the encircling crowd and the blocky figure of Kennicott's deputy, Jeff Wallis, pushed through. He surveyed the body of Sprewl and said: "What happened, Mark?"

The marshal repeated the information he had given Cartwright. When he was finished, Wallis said: "What happened to the brother? Where's he?"

"I told him to keep moving."

"You figure he'll do that?"

Kennicott shrugged. "Not much else I could do with him. No point in locking him up. Better to get him out of the country." He turned to a young boy, standing at his left hand. "Take my horse over to the stable, will you, Jimmy? Tell Leo to take care of him. He's had a hard trip."

"Leo ain't there," Wallis said. "Him and the rest of the committee is waiting at the jail to see you. That is, all but Jim and Humboldt here."

"Figured to wash up and eat first," Kennicott said. "However, if they're in a hurry, I guess I might as well get it over with. Let's go."

He started back up the dusty ribbon of street with Wallis at his side. A dozen steps ahead of him Jim Dry and the banker, Paris Humboldt, were preceding them.

"You know what they've got on their minds?"

Kennicott said: "Sure. I've got wind of it."

He glanced to his right, to the building standing on the corner that was Jergenson's Café. Alberta Heaston, her face a heart-shaped outline of paleness in the window, was watching him. He nodded and grinned, and she smiled back.

"Any trouble over Alberta Heaston working in Jergenson's place?" he asked.

"A little. The gambler at Carver's got a little mouthy, and I had to shut him up. A few others would like to get smart, but Jergenson's not taking any lip from them."

"Good. It might be a good idea for you to go over there now and eat. Be there when some of them show up for dinner."

Wallis nodded. "You figure you don't need me while you're jawing with that upright citizen's committee?"

Kennicott grinned. "If they want what I think they want, this won't take long. I'll join you in a few minutes."

Wallis said—"Fine."—and turned back toward the café.

Ahead of him Kennicott saw Dry and Humboldt reach and turn into his office at the jail. To have been waiting for him, as Jeff had said they were, they must be in a hurry to get things said. Well, he was ready for them, but he did hope one thing. He hoped the Reverend Lockridge was not with them. He was having a hard time holding his temper with Judith's father.

III

But the Reverend George Lockridge was there. Mark saw him as he entered the small room, a tall, darkly clad man with a severe, disapproving face. He would have something to say about the killing of Pete Sprewl before the hour was out. A newcomer to the country, he had no understanding of the frontier and the demands placed upon a lawman in keeping order.

Kennicott removed his wide-brimmed hat and tossed it onto his desk. He glanced about the room. They were all present, all the big men of the town. Jim Dry, short and fat with sweat laying a bright shine on his jowled face. White-haired Paris Humboldt. Keith Crandall, his sharp, cunning features expressionless. Next to him stood Leo Kane, youngest of the group. Kane ran the livery stable and blacksmith shop.

And finally there was Walker Rohle, acknowledged leader of

41

the committee. Rohle owned the Trail Queen, largest, gambling hall and saloon in Cameo Crossing, the Drover's Hotel, a fair-size ranch some miles west of the town, and had considerable interests scattered elsewhere. A handsome, well-dressed, suave man, his charm was undeniable.

Kennicott settled gently against the corner of his scarred desk and favored each one present with a brief glance. Sunlight reaching through the open doorway of the office touched the star pinned to his left breast.

"Well, gentlemen," he said in a slow drawl, "what's on your minds? I take it that it's important."

Rohle smiled. "It is, Marshal. Very important. But first of all we want to make something clear to you. We are not censuring you for the fine job you have done here in Cameo Crossing. We all realize it was a raw, rough place when you took on the task. And I, for one, feel that if you found it necessary to kill six men in getting the job done, then you were justified in so doing. . . ."

"Seven men, it now appears," George Lockridge interrupted. "Seven human beings shot to death. Murdered!"

Kennicott had stiffened perceptibly at Rohle's mention of the men he had been compelled to gun down during the course of the town's clean-up. It had been an unnecessary remark and he realized it was uttered only as a means for widening the chasm that lay between Judith's father and himself. An impatient anger began to show at the hard-cornered angles of his face and his eyes pulled down slightly. An answer, hot and scathing, formed on his lips. He choked it back. It was useless to try and explain such things to Lockridge; he imagined he still lived in the safe and comfortable areas of the East where law was a uniformed policeman walking a quiet street and death was an uncommon, shocking occurrence.

"I am sure the marshal was only doing his duty," Rohle said. "To be able to kill, unfortunately, is . . . or perhaps *was* a requirement of the job."

Kennicott did not miss the implication in Rohle's words. He said coolly: "Still is, if you want to know the facts. It was Sprewl or me."

"For what cause?" the minister said. "Why was it necessary to kill him?"

Still clinging to his temper, the lawman said: "My job is to protect the people in my community. I was doing just that. Pete Sprewl and his brother had moved in on Missus Heaston and her family. When I came on the scene, Pete was attempting to force Missus Heaston to do as he wished. When I stopped him, it led to gun play."

"You killed a man over that . . . that brazen woman! What else should she expect from men?"

Kennicott came off the desk in a slow, rising motion. His face was tight and the amber of his eyes glittered like glass. "For a man who preaches charity, you have some mighty strange ideas."

Walker Rohle lifted his hands in a gesture of pacification. "Now, hold on a minute. This is all beside the point and it's getting us nowhere. I'll state our case frankly, Marshal. We want you to ease up on things around here. Forget this iron-handed law that you have in effect."

Kennicott eased back onto the desk. He had been right. They were wanting him to open up the town, asking him to let down the bars for the sake of more profit. He shook his head slowly. "Maybe you don't realize what doing that might cost you. A lot more than you'd get out of it."

Jim Dry said: "Oh, come now, Mark. Times have changed."

Again Kennicott shook his head. "Times, perhaps. But not men. The kind we'd be up against never change. Not until they are dead."

"Possibly," Walker Rohle agreed. "I bow to your superior experience and knowledge in such matters. But I say, and my fellow business associates feel the same way, there's no longer any sense in keeping such a tight clamp on the town. Frankly our businesses are suffering. We need more customers. New customers to put new money in circulation."

Kennicott considered those words for a time. Then: "You're not thinking straight. Not any of you. You sure don't want this town thrown wide open again. You, Jim, and you, Crandall . . . you both know what a bunch of liquored-up trail hands can do to a town. If you've forgotten, let me remind you of the last time King Overmeyer and his crew of OX cowboys were here. Two men killed on the street. Six women manhandled by drunks. Every window in town shot out and Joe Medary's saloon burned to the ground. Is that the kind of new business you're looking for?"

There was a long silence, and then Jim Dry, stammering a little, said: "Well, no, of course not. But maybe they've changed now."

"Changed? Men like Overmeyer and his trail hands never change."

"There are other trail herds . . . ," Leo Kane ventured.

"Sure. Some not so bad, some maybe worse than OX. But all trouble, right down to the heels. I can promise you that for certain. And I'll tell you this. You'll never talk me into throwing this town open to the likes of that Texas bunch or any other. I drove them out once and I don't hanker for the job again. And if the mayor was in town, I think he'd back me up on that."

Walker Rohle shrugged, his shoulders moving only slightly under the fine broadcloth of his gray, knee-length coat. "Well, you are the law here, Kennicott. What you say goes for me. But I feel the merchants who have their hard-earned cash invested in the town should receive some consideration from you. After all, if we can't survive, the town won't, either. I think the mayor would agree to that, also."

There was a commotion in the doorway. Glancing up Kennicott saw the grizzled face of Jeff Wallis. The deputy said: "Marshal, you'd better come on over to the Trail Queen. Quick."

"The Trail Queen?" Rohle echoed, half turning. "Some trouble there?"

Wallis ignored the man. "There's a drunk getting out of hand. Pretty ugly about it."

"Can't you handle him?" Kennicott asked.

Wallis nodded. "Reckon I can. But he's packing a gun and your orders was to call you if anybody showed up around here wearing artillery."

Kennicott nodded. "That's right, Jeff." He reached for his hat. Pulling it on, he faced the delegation.

"We can go on with this later, if you say, but, as far as I'm concerned, the answer is no. The lid stays on. When the mayor gets back from Saint Louis, you can take it up with him."

Lockridge pushed suddenly forward, his eyes angry and snapping. "Now, see here, Kennicott. I think you're being unreasonable about this. I think these men have reason to complain because I don't believe things are as bad as you want us to think. Maybe it's not necessary to be so tough and hard. . . ."

"And maybe you don't know what you're talking about," Kennicott cut in, still remembering Lockridge was Judith's father. "You're a newcomer to this town. You don't know what it was like before. Right now it's a decent place for a man to raise his family. Three years ago it wasn't."

"That's what we're telling you," Lockridge said triumphantly. "You're talking about three years back. This is Eighteen Seventy-One. Times have changed for the better. Men are forgetting war and killing. This country is civilized now and no longer needs to be ruled by violence."

Kennicott wagged his head. Lockridge should know better. He was sure the others did, but the minister had not lived in the West long and perhaps had some excuse. He started to make an answer when his eyes caught the urgency on Jeff Wallis's face. There was no time to argue about it now—really no point in arguing it at all. He pushed through the half circle of men and walked to the doorway.

The minister's voice reached after him. "Gentlemen, I suggest we continue this discussion at the parsonage where we may find a little more comfort. Perhaps the marshal will favor us with his presence after he has finished with his duties."

Kennicott nodded. "I've said my feelings on the matter. If you want it repeated, I'll be glad to accommodate you. After I've taken care of the trouble at the Trail Queen and had a bite to eat, I'll be available."

Turning on his heel, he moved out into the day's bright sunlight.

IV

With Jeff Wallis at his side, Kennicott started down the street for the Trail Queen. Behind him he heard the delegation taking its leave, striking for the opposite direction, for the small, shingle-roofed house that stood beside the church. Judith would be there, he realized. She would hear them talking, hear what they would be saying about him. And she would also learn of Pete Sprewl's death and that it concerned Callie Heaston. And she would wonder about it. But she would wait until she heard it from him before she made up her mind. The Reverend George Lockridge was her father and he was forceful with his opinions, but Judith's mind was her own.

Through the haze of noonday heat Kennicott glanced over the town, *his* town, he had come to feel. It was a good place, lying near a plentiful supply of fine water, at the exact point where the main trails running to the four winds crossed. It had a future, he was sure. It could grow and become a city of importance, if given the chance. But that chance would never come if it reverted to the old law of gunpowder and violence. The steady influx of families would soon stop and eventually the migration would begin. And one day Cameo Crossing would find itself a shell of empty, deserted houses and buildings with only the heat and dust and lawless renegades prowling the streets.

His decision of a few minutes ago crystallized into a hard determination. Regardless of what Rohle and the others wanted, he wasn't going to let it happen. Not so long as he was able to make himself heard and use a gun. Cameo Crossing was a good town—and he owed that much to it.

His thoughts came back to the moment, to the business at hand. "Know this *hombre* at the Trail Queen?"

"Stranger to me," Wallis answered. "Somebody said his name was Billy Ringo. . . . Say, what was on the citizens' minds?"

Kennicott shrugged. "They want me to open up the town to the trail hands again. They say they need more business."

Jeff Wallis swore softly. "Why, the ding-dang' fools. They ought to know better'n that. Them trail-driven hellions will cost them ten times more'n they'll get back."

They reached the broad gallery of the Trail Queen and halted. Kennicott again surveyed the street, and then mounted the two steps. He crossed the porch to the scuffed doors, Wallis a step behind him. Thrusting the doors inward, he entered, hesitating only momentarily to allow his eyes to adjust to the change.

The saloon was nearly deserted at this time of day. Not more than half a dozen patrons were present and these were scattered well away from the bar, giving the hulking figure there wide berth. At Kennicott's entrance Alf Wisdom, the barkeeper, looked up quickly from something he was doing behind the counter.

"Don't want no trouble in here, Marshal," he said in a low

voice and eased away from his customer. Kennicott swept Wisdom with a cold glance. The man, he knew, was far more than just an employee of Walker Rohle's. He belonged to the saloon owner body and soul. "You're the one that sold him the whiskey," he said.

He moved forward to a point where he could better see the cowboy, a tough-looking, belted man with a week's or more growth of black beard obscuring his features.

"Appears you're a stranger around here," he said.

Billy Ringo lifted his bloodshot eyes. "You ever see me before?"

"Can't say that I have."

"Then I reckon I'm a stranger," Ringo answered. "What about it? Some law against bein' a stranger?"

"There's a law in this town about wearing a gun. You know about it?"

Ringo swung a hard grin about the room. "Seems like I did hear somebody mention it."

"Then what are you doing with that gun on? Why didn't you check it with the bartender?"

Ringo's eyes came to a halt on Kennicott. Some of the whiskey laxness seemed to have faded from him and the lawman had the sudden impression the man had not been as drunk as he pretended.

"I figure I'm old enough to do just as I please. What's more, I don't shuck my iron for nobody. And that includes tinhorn marshals."

"Around here you do," Kennicott said. "Either lay that gun up on the bar or I'm taking it off you and running you in."

Ringo's small, black eyes sparked. "Now," he drawled, "that could be a right smart of a chore."

"I've had tougher ones," Kennicott said.

The room was in absolute silence. Out in the street, there

were a few muted noises but within the high-ceilinged square of the Trail Queen there were no audible sounds except the breathing of men.

"Put that gun on the bar!" Kennicott said suddenly.

Ringo came halfway around. He rested his elbows on the counter and grinned lazily at the lawman. "Suppose you try liftin' it yourself, Marshal," he murmured. "Supposin' you try."

"Seems you're itching for trouble, Ringo."

"Somethin' you already got, Marshal."

Kennicott delayed no longer. His hand came up in a blurred arc. The muzzle of his heavy .45 pointed at Ringo's belly. Ringo's eyes spread a little in surprise at the speed of Kennicott's move and a trace of admiration flickered in their depths.

"Fast. Mighty fast," he murmured.

"Take that gun by the butt and put it on the bar," Kennicott commanded. "Two-finger hold and do it real slow."

Ringo's expression had returned to one of cool insolence. He reached for his weapon, moving deliberately, and plucked it from its holster. Raising it above the level of the counter, he let it drop with a clatter onto the polished surface.

"Now step away from it."

Ringo complied, never taking his eyes off Kennicott's face. The marshal turned to his deputy. "Collect the iron, Jeff."

Wallis yelled: "Watch him, Mark!"

Kennicott pivoted. He saw Ringo's hand plunging into the depths of his brush jacket, reaching apparently for a hidden pocket gun. He fired as he spun. Ringo jolted from the impact of the heavy bullet. He twisted half about and fell forward.

Kennicott remained where he stood, powder smoke coiling up about him in a thin, blue cloud while the thundering echoes of the shot bounced around the room. Alf Wisdom came from behind his counter and dropped to his knees beside Ringo. Kennicott watched him fumbling inside the man's coat, searching for the Derringer or whatever weapon it was he had been so desperately trying to reach. The saloon's other customers, shocked from their places along the far wall, pressed closer.

Wisdom straightened up. He thrust his hands into his side pockets and a frown crossed his square, florid face. "Dead as a pole-axed goat. Marshal, how come you to pull a stunt like that?"

Kennicott moved a step forward. "Meaning what?"

"Shooting a man down like that. Cold blood. Why, he didn't have a gun. Something you sure knew when you made him put his on the bar."

"He was going for an inside gun," Kennicott said coldly. "Didn't you find one?"

"Me? I was feeling his heart. Wanted to see if the poor feller was still alive. Didn't notice no inside gun."

Jeff Wallis slipped by Kennicott. He dropped beside Ringo and rolled him over. Carefully he searched the man's clothing, finding nothing.

In a voice that carried throughout the saloon Alf Wisdom said: "You just cut down an unarmed man, Marshal. That's what it amounts to. Made him lay down his iron and then murdered him."

Kennicott stared at the bartender. "You know better than that, Alf," he said sharply. "You saw him going into his coat after something."

Wisdom shook his head. "I didn't see nothin' like that, Marshal. Ringo had his back to me. Any you others see Ringo make a move to draw a gun?"

There was a murmur of noes. Of course they could not have seen it, Kennicott realized. They were across the room and at the man's back. But Wisdom should have been able to see what happened. He swiveled his attention to Jeff Wallis.

"He sure was reaching for something," the old deputy

declared. "I'd 'a' swore he had a little gun tucked away in a pocket somewhere."

Alf Wisdom smiled knowingly at his scatter of customers. "We would be expecting you to say that, Jeff. You lawmen always hang together, when something like this comes along."

Wallis muttered under his breath and took a step toward the bartender. Kennicott dropped a hand on his shoulder and halted him. There was something going on that he did not fully understand. Just what, he could determine later. Right at that moment there were other things to be taken care of.

"Forget it, Jeff. Go get Doc Cartwright."

Grumbling, the deputy wheeled for the doorway.

Kennicott backed up to the bar and hooked his elbows upon the edge. "Just everybody stay put," he said, "until the coroner gets here."

V

Cartwright, the curious townspeople in tow, bustled into the saloon, nodded to Kennicott, and dropped beside Ringo. After making an examination to assure himself the man was dead, he arose and moved to a nearby table where he sat down. Taking a fold of papers from his inside pocket, he flattened them carefully and with poised pencil said: "Anybody know this corkscrew's name?"

Alf Wisdom said quickly: "Billy Ringo."

"Just so," the medico said, and made notations on his paper. He glanced about and rapidly named half a dozen men to serve as jurors for the inquest. When this was done, he looked up and asked: "Now, what happened here?"

"The marshal shot him," Wisdom said.

Cartwright's sharp old eyes flickered to Mark Kennicott. He studied the tall lawman's face for a long minute, having his own deep thoughts on something. Then: "This one done in the line

Ray Hogan

of duty, too, Marshal?"

"Well, it was this way . . . ," Wisdom began.

Kennicott cut him off. "The man was drunk and creating a disturbance. He was carrying a gun that was against the law and also, to my way of thinking, was a dangerous character. I disarmed him."

"Disarmed him? Why shoot him then? Did he resist?"

"He made a move to get at something in his inside pocket. Near the left armpit. I figured it was a hidden gun and fired."

There was a murmur in the crowd. The bartender shook his head vigorously, indicating his disagreement.

Cartwright frowned. "Well? Was there a hidden gun?"

"No, sir, there sure wasn't," Alf Wisdom declared. "I didn't find one."

"You didn't find one." Cartwright's face turned quickly apoplectic. "What business have you got searching a dead body before the coroner arrives?"

Wisdom, crestfallen, looked down. "I was just feeling his heart, Doc. Wanted to see if he was dead. Ask Jeff Wallis there. He looked for a gun."

"I ought to have you arrested for interfering with the due process of law," Cartwright continued, ignoring the suggestion. "Damned nosey people," he added in a lower tone, drumming impatiently upon the table with his fingertips. Then: "What about it, Jeff? You find a gun?"

Wallis shook his head. "Didn't find one, Doc. But I sure thought he was going for one."

Cartwright considered that thoughtfully, weighing the statement in his mind. More people were coming into the Trail Queen now. Walker Rohle and Jim Dry and the stern-featured minister, George Lockridge. They took up places in the circle, just behind the doctor.

"How about the rest of you men who were here, present, in

52

the saloon . . . any of you see just what happened?"

"Couldn't see much, Doc," one of the patrons replied, pushing forward a step. "I saw this Ringo lay his gun up on the bar. The marshal was a-pointin' his hogleg straight at him. Then all of a sudden the marshal shoots and this Ringo flops over dead. That's the way it looked from where I was a standin'."

"Same here," a voice behind him chimed out. "This Ringo's back was to me, but I could sure see the marshal."

Walker Rohle moved into the center of the circle. Men fell back to give him room. Facing the doctor, he said: "What's the trouble here?"

Cartwright gave him a withering glance. "No trouble. A point of law, no more, no less."

"But a man lies there dead!" George Lockridge's outraged voice broke in. "That's considerably more than a mere point of law! Who did this terrible thing?"

Alf Wisdom said: "The marshal."

Lockridge whirled to Kennicott. His face was contorted, his eyes blazing. "You!" he shouted. "You again! Twice this day you have taken the life of a man. Have you no qualms at all when it comes to taking human life?"

"Maybe you better hear the facts first, Reverend," Cartwright broke in coldly. "You seem in a mighty powerful hurry to condemn a man without knowing first what happened."

"What facts could there be? There is no good reason for taking a man's life. Especially when one is a peace officer. And as to facts, don't those of the past and these of the present speak for themselves? I doubt if any of the eight men this . . . this executioner has killed needed to die."

"Possibly," Cartwright said icily, "it's a thing we're trying to decide about this Ringo now, if you will allow us to continue." He swung his attention to the men chosen as jurors. "The question before us is this . . . was the marshal justified in shooting the deceased Ringo? The marshal maintains he thought the deceased was reaching inside his coat pocket for a hidden gun. That thought was shared by his deputy."

"And nobody else?" Lockridge demanded.

"Nobody else was in position to see it," Cartwright explained patiently. "Everybody else was behind him."

Lockridge lifted his gaze to Kennicott. "Then we have only the word of a man who has already killed seven poor humans that this shooting was justifiable. That he did so in the performance of his duty. . . ."

"Now, hold on here!" Cartwright exclaimed angrily. "I'm run-. . . ."

". . . a man who refuses to believe there is any other way to administer the duties of his office except by bloodshed and death. A man who still lives by the ancient law of tooth and claw."

Kennicott's face was a stolid mask, hiding the anger riding through him in wild surges. Lockridge was a fool. He was Judith's father but he still was an ignorant fool for all his education and high calling. But he was a fool not for what he believed in but because he did not know whereof he spoke and thus was expressing broad opinions heedlessly. He dropped his glance to Cartwright, the impatience showing plainly in his taut features.

The doctor pounded his fist upon the table to command silence. Lockridge ceased his talking and the murmur of voices stopped. Looking about the crowd, Kennicott sensed the undercurrent of belligerence and animosity that had been generated against him.

In a stiff voice Cartwright said: "We're not here to listen to any sermons, Reverend. I'll be obliged if you'll save them till next Sunday. And what you've said has nothing to do with this case. Has no bearing whatsoever on it. Now, you jurors remember that. Excuse us now, Reverend. If you'll get the hell out of here, we'll get on with our jobs."

Lockridge stared at the medical man, his face flushing bright crimson. He turned suddenly on his heel and left the saloon, passing on through the swinging doors without a backward glance.

"Now we'll proceed," Cartwright announced, his voice filled with satisfaction.

Immediately Walker Rohle stepped forward to the doctor's improvised desk. He covered the circle of men with his engaging smile and ducked his head courteously to Cartwright.

"Mister Coroner, I am not a member of your jury but allow me to say, as a citizen of the town, I hardly think this inquiry need go further. We all have the utmost confidence in the ability and judgment of our marshal and I am sure, if he thought this man, Ringo, was attempting to draw a gun, he thought so honestly. Naturally he was entitled to shoot to protect his life, just as any man would be."

There was a ripple of approval through the crowd. Kennicott threw a quick look at Alf Wisdom. The bartender's mouth was half open, his eyes filled with surprise.

"What's another dead gunslinger, more or less?" a voice piped up from the back of the room.

"Exactly," Walker Rohle said, "though stated a bit cold-bloodedly. If I may suggest, Mister Coroner, I move we give Marshal Kennicott a clean bill on this matter."

There was another general murmur of approval. Cartwright banged on the table. "You're out of order, Rohle. You have no connection with this jury whatever. Nevertheless," he continued, facing his jurors, "I will entertain such a motion and verdict from you gentlemen."

He had it immediately, words parroted exactly to those of the smiling, confident Walker Rohle. Kennicott eyed the man closely. To have him exhibit such a show of kinship was not ordinary. They were friendly to a point of civility but there it stopped. Perhaps because of Judith there was no real friendship between them but there was also the fact that Mark Kennicott could never bring himself around really to trust the man.

". . . then we're agreed the deceased, name of Billy Ringo, met his death resisting arrest at the hands of a duly authorized officer of the law in the person of Mark Kennicott? And the said officer was justified in shooting the said Billy Ringo?"

The jury agreed and crowded up to sign the statement Cartwright had written on the paper. Rohle lifted his hand for silence.

"Now that this disagreeable business is done with, let's all have a drink. Move up to the bar, gentlemen." He nodded to the bartender. "Alf, this is on the house."

There was a general surge toward the lengthy mahogany counter. Cartwright motioned for two men to pick up Ringo's body and carry it to his office. Kennicott stepped aside to allow their passage, and then followed them into the street. He didn't want a drink at the moment. He was revolving the last few minutes' events about in his mind, trying to piece them together, make them fit. He was still unconvinced that Ringo was not trying to reach for another gun, and he was remembering Walker Rohle's defense of him and the look on Alf Wisdom's face when he did so.

There was something haywire but he could not place his finger on it. Maybe after he had washed up and shaved and had a bite to eat, he could think more clearly. Better still, he would talk it all out with Judith.

VI

Jeff Wallis, who had tarried within the saloon long enough to have a free drink on Walker Rohle, caught up with Kennicott before he had gone a dozen steps. The deputy was saying something to him but Kennicott was only half hearing; his thoughts were back in the smoke-filled, shadowy depths of the Trail Queen and he was remembering the way Doc Cartwright had looked at him and he was hearing again the low murmurings.

There had been accusation there. And blame. Some of it clearly open, some thinly veiled, and over it all the words of George Lockridge rode heavily, second only in their quality to irritate and disturb to Rohle's patronizing efforts on his behalf. He shook his head impatiently; he had acted honestly and as he had judged best; if there were some who chose to believe otherwise, that was their privilege.

He had never killed a man needlessly, never in his life as a lawman or before. Even during the four years of war it had been a matter of survival, just as it had been with Billy Ringo. He had thought Ringo was trying to pull a pocket gun on him and had acted accordingly; you did that automatically when you dealt with such men if you wanted to stay alive. You just could not take time to find out what a drifter like Ringo had in mind when he made such a move; you simply assumed he meant to kill you and you acted first.

And that was wrong, if you believed what the Reverend Lockridge said. You stood there and waited; maybe some twenty seconds later you realized the man was reaching for a sack of tobacco and the papers or possibly he meant to scratch himself, but most likely you wouldn't know anything for sure about it because you would be dead and only the bystanders would know he was going for a gun.

If you followed the minister's line of reasoning, you waited to be fully certain what a man had in mind. Only it wouldn't work when you were dealing with men like Billy Ringo and Pete Sprewl and the other six men now lying out on Boot Hill. You gave hardcases like any one of them the slightest edge, the merest chance, and one day the mayor would be looking for a new vest to pin the badge on while they took you for a slow ride down the main street.

He regretted the necessity for killing Ringo. It was never a pleasant task to blast out any man's life, however much he deserved it, and he never got over the feeling of being a little sick in the stomach when it was done with. But it was part of the job, a facet of the whole and a man accepted it when he agreed to the responsibilities of keeping law and order. The Billy Ringos were like weeds; they had to be cleaned out and cleared away before civilization could take root and grow in this frontier land. His was the job of doing just that.

He was vaguely aware of Jeff Wallis's voice. "Sure beats me. I figured that Ringo was going for a Derringer. Still ain't so sure he wasn't."

Kennicott came to a full stop. "Why?"

"You get a good look at Alf Wisdom while he was bending over Ringo? While he was feeling around under his coat? You see him plain?"

Kennicott shook his head. "Couldn't see at all. He had his back part way to me."

"Maybe you remember when he got up he had his hands in his pockets, or he was putting them there. Could be he found a Derringer and palmed it out of sight."

Kennicott said—"That's so."—in a thoughtful way. "But why? What reason would Alf have for doing it? Ringo meant nothing to him."

"But maybe getting you in trouble does. Don't forget Alf is a double-barreled, deep-dyed admirer of Rohle."

Kennicott shook his head. That didn't fit the puzzle, either. "If Rohle was trying to nail me to the wall, then why did he step in with his little speech? About all he had to do was keep shut up. Lockridge had done a pretty fair job of skinning me and the rest were willing to take it up from there."

"Could be," Wallis murmured, his wise old eyes vacant, "but there's no figuring Walker Rohle. He goes a long way around to reach the gate sometimes." He halted as a new thought reached his mind. "I reckon you realize none of this is going to do you any good with the parson's daughter and it sure's gonna put Rohle in strong, at least with him."

Kennicott nodded. "She's got a mind of her own. She will do her own deciding. You can figure on it, and all the talk he hands her won't change her."

"Sure can make you look bad, though. That Sprewl deal this morning, over the widow Heaston. And now Billy Ringo."

Kennicott let his gaze stray down the street toward the parsonage. Judith would have the story from her father by this time. Likely she was standing now in their parlor, calm and serene as she was always, her black hair shining as he remembered it, her deep blue eyes intent while she listened. Even though things had not been going so well for them lately, she would not be forming her opinion, not until she heard his side of the story.

Like her father she abhorred violence and bloodshed but, unlike him, she had some understanding for the necessities and demands of his profession. She realized no lawman could go untouched by the hard and brutal realities of his office; that there were things he must do and had been compelled to do in the past. Actually therein lay their differences; she would have it all in the past.

She would have him resign, forsake his job as town marshal. Get into some profession or business. Perhaps buy a ranch and become a cattle grower. Some less violent and dangerous way of life that would offer no such problems as the men lying now on Boot Hill. Only you never run out of their sort, no matter where you went or what you did. They were always around somewhere but he could not convince Judith of that truth.

To women life was a simple thing, it seemed to Mark Kenni-cott. A thing was black or it was white and with damned little shading in between. Many of the problems that beset a man, huge insurmountable things involving honor and duty and peace of soul, women often brushed lightly aside as unworthy of second thought. Life was what counted—life, security, and a man's safety from his enemies. They seemed never to understand there were other things that counted.

His thoughts came back to Jeff Wallis who was saying: ". . . and them tail-waggers with him, they'll jump when he hollers frog and be grinning like a 'possum eating honey when they do."

Idly he nodded to the deputy, the man's words making but small impression upon him. He could very easily lose Judith over this day's work, he knew. Feeling as she did about his way of life and, under the pressure of her father's words, she could come to some decision about their future. Not that she was incapable of making up her own mind without her father's influ-ence, but their near arguments about his resigning had grown more frequent of late and both were wearing a little thin on the matter. The deaths of Sprewl and Ringo could prove to be the final straw; it would be the culmination that brought him face to face with a choice.

And if it did? If Judith confronted him with a decision to forsake his profession or forsake her, what then? What would his answer be?

His gaze came back from the parsonage. He realized he and the deputy were standing near the middle of the street, that a few people were regarding them with curious interest.

He said: "Stick around the office, Jeff. I'm going to clean up and get a bite to eat. I'll be over later."

Wallis said—"Sure thing."—and moved off toward the jail.

Kennicott swung to his right, heading for his lodgings in a small structure just beyond the business buildings. He turned into the narrow passageway lying between adjoining buildings and came abruptly to a halt. The tall figure of a man had been standing at the far end—a man who looked very much like Curly Dan Sprewl.

Kennicott lunged into the narrow corridor and raced to its end. He came out into the alley behind the buildings and stopped, his hand resting on the butt of his gun. There was no one in sight. If there had been someone there, if it had been Curly Dan, he had disappeared completely.

VII

Walker Rohle's quarters in the Trail Queen reflected the man's character. Scorning the ground floor with its traffic and noise, he had taken the two front rooms on the second level, knocked out the intervening wall, and converted them into an apartment of spacious elegance. He had furnished it with heavy, ornate furniture, half as a bedroom and half as an office from which he oversaw and managed his varied business interests.

Thick carpeting covered the floor, muffling the uplifting din beneath. A well-stocked bar complete even to a crystal-clear back mirror graced one wall of the office half, which was separated from the bedroom by braided leather portieres. The walls supported several large pictures, both prints and oils; one was a scene along the Mississippi River, another the portrait of a Union officer resplendent in his uniform and medals. There was another of a blonde woman staring pensively down from her side-saddle perch upon a white stallion.

It was a long step to that small town in Ohio where Walker Rohle had been born, a vast difference in the man who had departed that somnolent village just prior to the war to make his way in a burgeoning world. He had done a brief stint in the ranks of the Union forces but it had been of small consequence; he was far too busy with matters pertaining to his own welfare to care one way or another about idealistic causes. They were for those who could afford them; he could not for he had a fortune to accumulate.

And in seven years he had done just that. Possessing that faculty for always being in the right place at the right time he had prospered magnificently and the day he had ridden into Cameo Crossing money had ceased to be an objective in his life. There was nothing left now but to live and enjoy, no goal remaining except to grow old gracefully in complete luxury.

But the make-up of Walker Rohle was such that it could not be so, that it was an impossibility to lie dormant. Before he scarcely knew what had happened, the surging, growing spirit of the widening frontier land had seeped into his blood and he had become a part of it. He purchased land, built buildings, went into business, and one day found himself an all-powerful factor in a town destined, by geographical accident, to become important.

To further complicate and becloud a future he had once thought settled, another change took place. Judith Lockridge came to live in Cameo Crossing. In the past he had little time for women, but from the day he had first seen her walking down the street with her grimly intent father, he had known she was the one woman for him. That during the months following she had received him with all cordiality but seemed to prefer the company of Mark Kennicott was of no consequence. No good thing came easily and in the end he would win her over. He always accomplished those things he set forth to do.

Then it would be complete. He would be the nominal master, possessing not only Cameo Crossing, but Judith as well.

He stood now at the large front window and looked down upon the street below. Only a few people were abroad for the afternoon's heat lay fully upon the town. Lifting his gaze he could see the jail, Mark Kennicott's jail. The marshal was no fool; he knew that now. He would be thinking about the events at the Trail Queen and wondering what it all added up to.

The whole day had been one of fortunate accidents for Rohle. The killing of that drifter, Sprewl or whatever his name was, with the widow Heaston mixed in for added measure. That wouldn't help Kennicott any with Judith, who, according to her father, was about to break off with the marshal. And then Billy Ringo, an unknown apparently looking to build his reputation by shooting a lawman. Alf Wisdom had used his head when he hid the Derringer that had been in Ringo's shirt pocket. It made it look bad for Kennicott, and that was necessary for Rohle's plans to succeed.

Those incidents fitted in nicely with the ideas he had instilled in the Reverend Lockridge's mind, those tiny grains of poison that were suddenly flourishing so well. No matter what Cartwright's verdict had been on the death of Ringo, you would never convince Lockridge that Kennicott had not killed in cold blood, that he was a murderer at heart.

As to the other merchants he had no problem there. They were in the hollow of his hand; they would follow his lead and do exactly as he said. His promise of gold flowing into their tills was enough to convince them and bring them around to his point of view. Greed was an all-powerful motivation.

They could have the gold, the new wealth he planned to bring to Cameo Crossing. He was playing for higher, far more important stakes—for Judith and the town itself. Those were the only things that mattered now, and they were both almost within his grasp. Sentiment was swinging to him and Mark Kennicott might as well have been felled by Billy Ringo's hand; he soon would be that dead so far as the town and Judith were concerned. But he needed to act quickly. He must pick up and tie all the loose strings while the wind still blew right. Besides, King Overmeyer and his crew would be riding in tomorrow. All must be ready for them.

He moved back from the window to his desk, a broad, heavily carved affair imported from Mexico. It had cost a pretty penny, the freighting and all, but like everything else in his apartment, it was worth it. He enjoyed watching the expressions on other faces when they first beheld it; it probably cost more than most of them made in several years of hard work. Reaching under one corner he pressed a hidden spring release and a shallow drawer popped open. Into it he dropped the Derringer that Wisdom had taken from Billy Ringo. He pushed the drawer closed and went out onto the, narrow balcony that overlooked the bar.

"Alf!" he called to the bartender. The man glanced upward. "Find McCoy and send him up here."

He turned away without waiting for a reply, and took up a stand just outside the door of the apartment. McCoy, a young cowboy with a long scar running down his left cheek, came up the stairs hurriedly. McCoy was ambitious. He had dreams of being Rohle's right-hand man. He was as close to a hired gunman as Rohle had ever had. Rohle said: "Clete, go tell Kane and Crandall and Jim Dry I want to see them. Right away."

McCoy ducked his head. "How about the banker?"

"Never mind him," Rohle replied, and turned into his quarters. No use bringing up Humboldt. He would express no opinion one way or another, just so much deadwood to have around. When he saw what the others did, he would fall right in line.

He moved to the bar, thinking then of Clete McCoy. It might be wise to have a talk with him, take him on full time as a sort of bodyguard. Things might get a little touchy around town in the next day or two. Most likely he would come out of this episode with a few who did not feel so kindly toward him; Mark Kennicott particularly could be a serious threat. But he was not too sure of McCoy's capabilities. He needed a good man, one like Dave Seringo who worked for King Overmeyer. He had a far-reaching reputation and men gave him the walk when he came down the street. That was the sort of man he needed; maybe he should have a talk with Seringo when he got in town, hire him away from Overmeyer. He was thinking of that when a knock came at the door.

He moved to the door and twisted the knob. It was Leo Kane and Jim Dry. He motioned for them to enter and said: "Crandall?"

"He'll be here in a minute," Dry answered, and stopped at the bar. He looked inquiringly at Rohle, who nodded. Dry then poured himself a measure of bourbon, downed it, and smacked his lips. "Only time a man can get a drink of good whiskey is when he comes up here."

Rohle shrugged. "Good whiskey is wasted on the sort of customers Alf has downstairs. Anytime you want a quart of my stock, let me know."

Crandall arrived a few minutes later, breathing hard from the run up the back steps. He accepted his tumbler of liquor that Rohle poured, and then sat down on the deep leather-covered couch beside the other two merchants. Rohle took his own chair behind the Mexican desk and stared at his own glass of untouched whiskey. This would require careful maneuvering, he knew, to make it appear natural.

"I am assuming you have all heard of the unfortunate killing that took place down below a few minutes ago," he said finally. He was choosing his words, spacing them for their utmost effect. "The marshal was compelled, so the coroner and his jurors decided, to kill a man. Another killing took place earlier in the day, the details of which we do not know too well."

Jim Dry, always quick to sense the trend of Rohle's thinking, added: "And a pretty raw deal for the man, too. They say he wasn't even armed. Anybody's guess about the shooting this morning."

"The way I heard it, the shooting of this Ringo," Leo Kane broke in, "was that Kennicott thought he was going for a pocket gun inside his coat."

"Thought . . . that's the correct word," Rohle pointed out softly. "The marshal only thought he was. Nobody else saw Ringo make such a move. Now, this is the thing we are deploring, the one thing that is giving our town a bad name."

"I don't know," Kane protested in a doubtful voice, "if this Ringo, as they called him, did make such a move, we can't blame Mark for shooting him down."

"Like Walker says," Dry insisted, "nobody else saw Ringo go for a pocket gun. Nobody but Jeff Wallis, and you can't expect him to do anything but back his boss. Anyway, they didn't find a pocket gun on Ringo and that's proof enough for me."

"Me, too," Crandall said.

"Then you figure Kennicott was lying about it? That he just plain murdered Ringo for the hell of it?"

Walker Rohle's smooth voice cut into the argument. "I don't think we need to concern ourselves with that, men. Maybe Kennicott actually *thought* he saw Ringo reaching for a gun. Men who live by a gun are jumpy in such moments. Our coroner and a jury of citizens say he was justified in doing it, and, as far as I'm concerned, I accept it. We've got to stand behind our town officials no matter how we might feel personally. We must remember that without laws and the observance of them, we have nothing short of anarchy and that applies right here in Cameo Crossing the same as it does everywhere else."

"That's right, Walker," Jim Dry said, nodding his head vigorously. "We've got to go by the laws."

Rohle sipped his whiskey. "I believe that sincerely. That's why I acted as I did when the inquest began to get out of hand. I believe the marshal did what he believed was right under the circumstances but . . ."—Rohle paused again, balancing his words for effect again—"I think it is the last time we should let Kennicott compromise our principles."

There was a lengthy silence broken finally when Kane said: "What does that mean?"

"It means that, in my honest opinion, Kennicott has become a cold-blooded murderer behind his badge, that we no longer dare keep him around as our town marshal."

"You're right, Walker," Dry said.

"You mean take his badge? Fire him?" Crandall asked.

Rohle made a gesture with his hands. The large diamond on his left hand flashed brightly in the afternoon sunlight streaming in through the open window. "That's a harsh word, Keith. And it is something only the mayor can do."

"Then how . . . ?"

"I propose we, as the largest merchants in town, consider ourselves as councilmen assembled in emergency session to take action at once. We ask Kennicott to resign and, if he will not, suspend him."

"Suspend or fire, what's the difference?" Crandall murmured.

"In my opinion he will resign," Rohle continued. "He has resisted our efforts to open the town up as an aid to business, but now, after these two unfortunate killings this morning, he has placed himself at a considerable disadvantage. He has proved our point, so to speak . . . and the contentions of George Lockwood."

"What contentions?" Leo Kane demanded. "What's he know about things around here?"

"He says there have been too many killings, too much violence in the background of this town. Most of it, if not all of it, unnecessary. It is a harsh statement, one I do not fully agree with. In the past strong measures were necessary. But today it is a different story and we have killings that are uncalled for."

Keith Crandall got to his feet suddenly. He walked to the bar and refilled his glass, drifted back to the window. Looking down onto the street, he said: "You really think Mark has turned killer?"

His tone carrying the precise tone of regret, Rohle answered: "I'm afraid so, Keith."

"Well, this Ringo deal proves it to me," Jim Dry declared. "Two of them against the one. And him with no gun. Hardly need no more proof than that."

"Could be that's what is hurting business, sure enough," Crandall said then. "And if so, we ought to do something about it. I don't know if he'll resign or not, though."

"Kennicott is a smart man and I think he may be realizing he has jumped the track as a lawman," Dry said. "He may welcome the chance to quit. Killing sometimes gets to be a habit and a damn' hard one to break for a man who has authority to kill."

"Then let's put it up to him and get done with it," Crandall said, wheeling from the window. "Who'll we stick in his place? Jeff Wallis?"

Rohle made a delaying motion. "Now, hold on a bit. Let's not get too far ahead of ourselves. Let's be sure we're all agreed on this. We want to bear in mind that as emergency council members we represent the largest business interests of the town, but we do not speak for everybody. There undoubtedly will be many who figure we've done the wrong thing."

"That's right," Dry said. "Can't please everybody, that's for sure."

"You mean we ought to take a vote around town?" Crandall wondered.

"Yes, we should. That would be the best thing to do. " Rohle paused, giving the answer time to register. "But the trouble is, we don't have that kind of time. We've got to act today, now, before we have another Billy Ringo affair."

"Then how are we going to do it?" Crandall asked.

"By going to the Reverend Lockridge with the problem. I think we can safely assume he speaks for the majority of the townspeople. Leave it up to him. If he agrees with us, we can conclude the idea is generally agreeable."

"And if the rest of the town doesn't like it," Kane observed dryly, "it will be Lockridge's neck, not ours."

Rohle's cool glance settled upon the stable owner. He smiled faintly. "Exactly. But do you have a better idea?"

"Walker's right, Leo," Crandall said at that point. "We've got to act now, for the good of the town as well as for ourselves. Personally I figure the town will be satisfied, no matter what happens, so long as we appoint another marshal first off. And they all like Jeff Wallis."

"Jeff's too old for that job and you know it," Kane retorted. "Why don't we just go talk with Kennicott again and ask him to open the town up a little. Maybe he will if we lay the whole thing out before him. Show him how bad we're hurting. He's a hell of a good man to shuck."

"I agree with that," Rohle said quickly. "And I'm perfectly willing to try again, if you all figure it's the thing to do. But you will recall his attitude when we broached him earlier today. What makes you think he'll change his mind?"

Dry wagged his head. "I know Mark Kennicott. Once he's made up his mind, he won't change it. We better go along with Walker's idea."

"I vote for that," Crandall said. "We'll ask him to quit. Then, if he won't, we'll suspend him."

"Three of us are agreed," Rohle said. "How about you, Kane? You with us?"

Kane studied his knuckles. "Seems to me we're in an all-fired rush," he said slowly. "But, all right, I'll ride along with the rest. Let's get it over with."

Rohle's eyes flickered briefly. It had been easier than he had figured; he had expected more opposition from Leo Kane and possibly Crandall, but they had followed neatly along the lines he had drawn. And thinking back upon it, each would realize he had as much to do with the final decision to get rid of Kennicott as any other one. All that was left was to wind it up with George Lockridge, and he certainly would find no trouble at that point. The minister's attitude on the matter of Mark Kennicott was a foregone conclusion.

"I suggest we go to the parsonage at once and talk this all over with Lockridge," Rohle said, rising. "When we have come to our final decision, which depends, of course, on what the reverend thinks, we can send for the marshal."

It would be simpler to call in Kennicott and tell him right then he was through, finished in Cameo Crossing, once and for all time, Rohle thought as he moved toward the door with the three merchants. Only you didn't handle things that way. Not if you wanted to come out without any scars. Instead, you maneuvered carefully, systematically; you played people to the best advantage, one against the other, led them into making decisions you planted in their minds by clever conversation. And when it was all over with, you had what you wanted.

It was a very satisfying game. And a rewarding one.

VIII

Near the middle of the afternoon Mark Kennicott, much refreshed after a shave, a bath in the barbershop's tin tub, and a change of clothing, came again into the street. He paused beneath the overreaching porch of Hasselman's Dry Goods Store, feeling the hot breath of afternoon's heat striking at him with full force. There was no one abroad and over beyond the town, on the flat prairie land to the east, several dust devils were spinning brown funnels toward the empty sky.

He was thinking of Curly Dan Sprewl, of the fleeting glimpse he had had of a man standing at the far end of an alleyway—had it been Curly Dan? It did not seem likely; yet, being a practical man with little imagination and good eyesight, he could hardly have been wrong. Of course, it possibly was someone who resembled Sprewl; tall, thin cowboys were certainly not uncommon, and most men dressed very much alike. He considered that solution for several minutes, finally accepting it with some reservations. He hoped it was the answer, at any rate. He wanted no more trouble with Curly Dan—or any other man. He had seen enough bloodshed that day.

He moved out to the edge of the porch, scanned the street absently, and then crossed over to Jergenson's Café. Pulling back the dust-blotted screen door, he entered, heading for a table near a side window where a trace of breeze off the river offered more comfort. He drew out the chair, sat down, and glanced up to see Alberta Heaston, standing before him.

She apparently had been doing something near the stove for her face was flushed from the heat and there was a dampness alongside her pert nose. She had caught up her blonde hair with a wide ribbon to keep it in place and standing there, as she was, she reminded him very much of her mother except there was in her features a strength of character that was lacking in the delicate, doll-like face of Callie Heaston.

"So you've become a working girl," he said with a grin.

She smiled and then, at once serious: "I heard about the shootings. I'm glad you're all right."

Kennicott shook his head, not wanting to talk about it. "You like it here with Jergenson?"

"I like it fine. It's good to be working at something you get

71

paid for. He practically lets me run the place. Goes off and just turns it over to me. I'm cook, dishwasher, waitress, and everything else."

Kennicott did not share her enthusiasm. "Not a good idea," he murmured. "I'll speak to Jergenson about it."

"Oh, no, Mark!" she cried hastily. "Don't! He might not let me stay if he thought it would cause trouble."

"Does it?"

"Nothing I haven't been able to handle. There are a few men . . . but, of course, there always are. I'll be all right."

"I hope so," Kennicott said with a sigh. "I'm not for this idea, Alberta. I wish you wouldn't do it, but your ma said you had made up your mind. Just be careful. That's all I ask."

"Of course," she replied softly. "Would you like something to eat?"

"The usual. Steak, potatoes, coffee. And some of Jergenson's apple pie."

"It's my pie now." She laughed, going back behind the partition that separated the kitchen from the serving area. "I made it."

"Fine," Kennicott said. "I'll probably want a couple of pieces. . . ."

Kennicott had the hunger of a healthy man, and, when the platter was set before him, he fell to. Alberta hovered over him, refilling his coffee cup, bringing more warm bread, adding to the fried potatoes while he ate steadily. When at last he was finished, he pushed back his chair and reached for his tobacco and papers.

"Best meal I've had in months," he said. "If you cooked that, you ought to go out and start your own eating place. You're wasting your time here working for Jergenson."

Alberta's eyes were shining and there was a tenderness in their depths. "A girl doesn't learn to cook for business reasons," she said. "She learns so she can cook for a husband when she marries."

Kennicott fashioned his smoke and struck a match to it. "Lucky man," he said.

Alberta paused in her chore of stacking his dishes. She stared at him intently for a long moment, words seemingly about to come from her lips, words that matched the tenderness in her eyes. But after a time she shrugged, smiled faintly, and went on with her task.

Kennicott got to his feet. "Guess I'd better be getting on the job." He fished around in his pocket and came up with several coins. He laid a silver dollar on the table for his meal. "Is it all right to tip the waitress?"

Alberta shook her head. "It is not," she stated flatly. "At least, where you're concerned."

The screen door closed softly and a voice said: "Sure nice to be special people. Get a lot of extra attention from the help, eh, Marshal?"

Kennicott turned. It was Clete McCoy, one of Walker Rohle's hands. He nodded briefly, and reached for his hat.

McCoy said: "Rohle wants to see you. Over at the parson's."

"He send you after me?"

McCoy nodded without looking at him. His eyes were upon Alberta Heaston. "Speaking of special attention," he said to the girl, "how about me driving you home tonight? I'll get a buggy from Kane. . . ."

Alberta said quietly: "No, thank you. My mother will be in after me. I'll go with her."

"Well, now, maybe I can get somebody to ride with your ma. Then we. . . ."

Kennicott said: "You heard her, Clete. Forget it."

"Don't figure this is any of your business, Marshal. No harm in a man asking a girl to go for a ride." He stopped, a sly grin crossing his scarred face. "Or maybe it is your business. You got some special interest lately in the Heaston family, I hear. Real special . . . and mighty satisfactory, too, I reckon."

The combined and concentrated anger and exasperation for all the Billy Ringos, Pete Sprewls, Curly Dans, Clete McCoys, and their like suddenly exploded within Kennicott. His right hand came up in a swift arc. His knotted fist caught McCoy alongside the head. The smirking gunman went rocking sideways and crashed into the wall of the building, setting up a rattling of china and tinware.

"Damn you!" McCoy yelled, and reached for his gun.

Kennicott hit him again, driving him into the wall a second time. McCoy's head struck the wooden paneling hard and his eyes rolled. Kennicott stepped up against him and pulled the pistol from its holster, thrust it into his own waistband. Grasping the man by the arm, he shoved him toward the door and out into the street.

"Cool off," he said in a harsh voice. "And you know the law about wearing guns in this town. I'll just hang onto this one. Don't get another."

McCoy, his reeling senses, recovered, stared at Mark in suppressed fury. He seemed about to make some reply, thought better of it, and struck out across the street for the Trail Queen.

Kennicott turned to Alberta Heaston, standing just inside the screen door. "He gives you any more trouble, I want to hear about it. Job or no job."

The girl nodded silently, her face bright with the excitement of the moment.

Kennicott grinned at her and headed for Lockridge's. He had hoped to talk with Judith but it appeared that would have to wait again.

IX

The incident with Clete McCoy had not given Mark Kennicott any spare time to consider Rohle's summons. He thought of it now as he walked through the street's loose dust in the afternoon's late heat. It could mean but one thing; they were not accepting his refusal to open up the town. They intended, in some way, to force his hand. A wave of impatience swept through him. Maybe he should let them have their way. Maybe he was looking at it all wrong, worrying over a town and a lot of people who possibly didn't give a rap, one way or another about him.

Instead, perhaps he should be thinking of himself, listening to Judith and planning for his own happiness with her. Let Rohle and his crowd have the town, take it over, and do what they willed with it. He and Judith could find a new life elsewhere, as she wished they might. He regretted again that he had not been able to talk with her before this meeting. He could have straightened out a few things in his mind if he had.

He reached the low, shingle-roofed structure, and paused. He searched the porch hopefully. Judith might be there, waiting for him, and they could have a few moments alone. She was there, standing just within the door, tall and slim in a pale blue dress that fitted her figure closely. Her face was serious.

She came at once into his arms, returning his kiss. "I've been so worried," she said in a low voice.

He grinned. "About me? You know better than that."

"I tried to see you earlier. . . ."

He shrugged. "Same here but it seems there's a lot of things going on today. Meetings and the like."

"I heard about the trouble at Callie Heaston's."

The tone of her voice brought his sharp glance to her. "You heard what about it?"

"That you were out at her place. That you killed a man over her."

For a long minute he did not answer. Then: "You believe that's the way it was?" His voice was stiff and he was looking beyond her, to the deserted street.

"I'll believe what you tell me," she said.

His shoulders went down, expressing his relief. "It wasn't that way at all, Judith. . . ."

"Marshal." The clipped voice of George Lockridge cut in from behind them. "We're waiting."

Kennicott nodded. Judith moved a step closer to him. In a low voice she said: "Mark, they're all against you. Please do as they say. For my sake, if no other reason."

Kennicott smiled and touched her arm reassuringly. "Don't worry about it," he said.

He wheeled and followed Lockridge into the small, stuffy parlor, steep with late shadows, close with its trapped heat. Crandall, Dry, and Leo Kane were seated. Walker Rohle stood in the bay window. As Kennicott entered, he half turned and nodded in his pleasant, friendly fashion.

Kennicott halted in the room's dead center and let his gaze drift from one man to another. He was remembering Judith's words. What did they have in mind?

He said: "You wanted to see me?"

There was a moment's hesitancy as if none of those present wished to answer his question. Then Lockridge swung and faced him squarely. "We did," he stated crisply. "Kennicott, we're asking for your resignation."

The impact of the words struck Kennicott with the buffeting force of a winter wind. He stood rooted, momentarily speechless. First they wanted him to open up the town, throw it wide open to the wolves, and now, when he refused, they wanted to get rid of him entirely. By God, he had news for them. He wouldn't do it. They could all go to blazes. He simply wouldn't do it.

But in that next moment he was hearing Judith's words again—*For my sake, if for no other reason.*—and was remembering the hope in her dark eyes, the appeal for a life of their own. And suddenly he was sick and tired of it all, of the ceaseless battle to hold off the Billy Ringos on one hand and the people he had sworn to protect on the other.

He swung back to Lockridge. Oddly enough he did not feel too bitter toward the minister. The man simply did not know any better and had been led to believe the wrong things. With Rohle and the others it was a different matter. They *did* know. They had seen wide-open towns, towns that had been treed by trail hands and they were leading Lockridge on a snipe hunt when they made him think it couldn't happen again in Cameo Crossing.

"I hope you know what you're doing," Kennicott said after a time. "Mind telling me what brought this notion on? Because I wouldn't let down the gates, that it?"

"Not entirely," Lockridge replied. "We've simply come to the point where we can no longer accept you and your methods of law enforcement. These senseless killings today decided it for all of us."

"Those senseless killings, as you term them, were in the line of duty."

"Of course, of course. The coroner had to clear you. There was no other choice. It would never do to admit publicly our law officer was no more than a murderer hiding behind his badge of authority."

Kennicott's face drained of color. His tall shape seemed to grow even taller and his shoulders stiffened as the opaqueness of his eyes increased. The room became deathly still.

Walker Rohle's calm voice broke the tense hush. "I don't

believe Mister Lockridge means that exactly as it sounds," he said. "His language is a bit harsh only because he feels so strongly on the matter of violence. Now, as I see it, what's done is done, and all the talking in the world is not going to undo it. We had best forget it. All of us. And to simplify that, Marshal, we are agreed that your resignation is the key."

Some of the anger had dwindled from Kennicott when Rohle finished speaking. "One thing I'd like to know," he said, "is this an idea of everybody's, or just you four?"

"We represent the merchants and businessmen," Rohle answered easily.

"And I represent the people of Cameo Crossing in general," Lockridge added. "I speak for them."

"Do they know that?"

"I will take the responsibility of saying I do," the minister said stiffly. "The day of bloodshed is over for them and this town. A day they have long hoped for."

Kennicott smiled thinly, a bitter, hard corner grin that reflected his scorn. And his pity. "You've got a big surprise coming, Reverend. And a mighty sad one."

He turned his attention to the other men. "I'm being railroaded in this and I know it. But I don't care. I'm sick of all you. But before I'm through, I want to hear it from you direct." He halted his gaze upon Crandall. "You believe all this that's been said, Keith? Is this the way you want it?"

Crandall dropped his eyes and nodded. "We all decided, Marshal."

"Hardly necessary whether we believe it or not," Rohle said before he could question the other two men. "You proved the point today. Killing two men."

"That's right, Mark," Jim Dry said. "Looks like you wrote your own ticket."

Lockridge stirred impatiently. "This is taking up a lot of time.

78

How about it, Kennicott?"

Kennicott, surprisingly calm for the moment, said: "You want my job, you've got it. And I hope you have a fine time picking up the pieces of this town after the owlhoots and trail hands get through taking it apart."

"Don't worry about that," Crandall said at once. "We'll have a good marshal on the job."

"One who will believe in law enforcement without guns and bloodshed," Lockridge added.

Kennicott stared at the man. In a voice pitched to near exasperation, he said—"How any man can be such a fool. . . ."— and stopped. What difference did it make now? It was no concern of his. He had done his best for these people and now they chose to throw it all away. He swung about. "I'll be in my office when you're ready to take over."

Lockridge nodded. "Good. We will write out a resignation for you to sign and bring it to you."

Kennicott made no answer. He crossed the room to the front door, hoping Judith would be waiting on the porch. As he reached for the knob, he heard a step behind him. He paused, looked back. It was Lockridge.

"One thing more," the gaunt minister said, "you'll have nothing to do with my daughter. I forbid you seeing her again from this time on. Is that understood?"

Kennicott gave him a dry smile. "That's something we'll leave up to Judith," he said, and moved on into the yard.

X

Kennicott angled across the street in long strides. Cameo Crossing was beginning to come alive at the late afternoon hour as people began to do their necessary chores and shopping in the increasing coolness.

He reached the jail and was relieved to find it empty and Jeff

Wallis elsewhere at the time. He wanted to be alone with no questions to be answered, at least until he could again put his thoughts into an orderly condition. He tossed Clete McCoy's gun onto the rack near the window, dropped into his chair, and cocked his feet upon the battered desk.

He was recalling the day nearly three years gone when he had ridden into the town, when they had needed him and welcomed him and his fast gun and his willingness to walk in where others had feared to tread. They were happy when, one by one, he rid the place of the vermin, drove off the sharp gamblers, and exterminated the elements that were turning Cameo Crossing's existence into a bloody nightmare.

"Killer's Crossing" most people had termed it in those days. There was no questioning him then, no doubting his methods or his word. Nor did anyone hint he was a bloodthirsty killer hiding behind a star. Then it had been best wishes and slaps on the back and wholehearted encouragement for the task he was accomplishing. Everyone recognized his problems and stood foursquare behind him and the things he found necessary to do—three years ago.

Walker Rohle with his elegant ways and smooth tongue had not been heard of. And George Lockridge and Judith also were unknown, to arrive over two years later. But the others had been there then: Dry, Crandall, Leo Kane, Humboldt, and all the others. They could remember what the town was like before he completed cleaning it up and nailing down a tight lid upon it. After that, they all had said, it was a decent place in which to live and raise a family.

They could remember it, only they chose to forget. Could that mean he was wrong? Was that proof he had turned killer and they were justified in asking for his star?

Turned restless by that thought, he got to his feet and for a time moved about the small office, touching this, kicking idly at that, pausing to study some of the Wanted dodgers nailed to the wall. He was no wanton killer, no matter what they thought. In his own heart he knew it. He had not killed Billy Ringo without provocation, or Pete Sprewl, or any of the others. That was just something they were using to force the issue, to convince Lockridge and the others.

So be it. It didn't matter anyway. If they wanted him out, and they most certainly did, it was all right with him. Let them pin his badge on a straw man and instruct him to look the other way when outlaws and tinhorn gamblers and the wild bunches started flocking into town. And come they would, just as fast as the news got around. To his way of thinking, it meant the end of Cameo Crossing's future—not because he would not be there, but because there would be no real law to hold them in check.

And Walker Rohle and the others knew that! But they were not worrying about it. All they were considering was the present, ignoring the past, refusing to look at what the future would hold. Profits, that was their by-word. More money for themselves—and to hell with what comes after.

He wondered then about Judith, hearing again the words of her father. Would she heed him, believing him and the others? It would be tough to leave alone, to go without her. He had come to picture the future only with her at his side, as his wife, making all things complete. Many a night he had sat his horse on the crest of an outlying hill and studied the lights of the houses, watching them wink out one by one, dreaming of and planning for the day when he would have such a home. A home like other men with a wife—Judith—waiting to welcome him. Was that, too, a lost hope?

"Mark!"

He had not heard her come to the door but her voice was like a sudden shaft of light breaking through a black night. He whirled and came to his feet.

"Oh, Mark!" she cried, and ran to him.

He folded her into his arms, astounded yet relieved.

He held her close, feeling the softness of her against him, savoring the sweet perfume of her hair, lying tightly upon his face.

"I was afraid you might be gone . . . without me."

Gently he took her by the shoulders and held her at arm's length. "I didn't know if it mattered. Didn't you want me to go?"

"Not without me, you know that. You weren't going to leave without me."

He stared at her through the gathering shadows of the room. "After this day's work I thought things might be finished between us. For all time."

"Oh, men are so blind! When you told them you would resign, it was the answer to my prayers. It was everything I had hoped for, Mark. More, even. You will never know of the worry I have had for you in these past months."

"Worried over me? Is that what has been on your mind?"

"Day and night. Every time I saw you start down the street, I wondered if you would come back, or if some gunman's bullet would cut you down from the darkness."

Kennicott shook his head. "Your father doesn't think such things will happen here in Cameo. He believes the day has come when. . . ."

She laid her finger upon his lips to still him. "Please don't hate him too much, Mark," she said gently. "He is a good man, sincere in all he does, and he believes everything he speaks. Whether he is right or wrong, I don't know, and I suspect only the future can say. But he is my father and he has always been good to me."

He said: "Being your father he will have my respect. But there it ends. You must know that, Judith. I'll have no secrets between us on that score. He can get a lot of good people hurt saying and doing what he thinks is right when he knows nothing about it."

She took his face between her hands and kissed him again. "Never mind. It's no concern of ours now. All such is behind us. We'll leave this place and find a new life in a new country. A place where every moment won't be torture for me and I won't be filled with dread and worry that I may never again see you walk through a doorway."

"I'm a lawman, Judith. It's part of my job to take chances."

"But you don't have to be a lawman. You can do other things. Maybe we can buy a small ranch. Or start one of our own."

"It takes money to do that. I doubt if I could scrape up enough cash to buy a dozen cows much less a full-grown spread."

"With what I have saved we will have enough to do something. We'll manage somehow. The main thing is that you will be away from this terrible life of guns and death. You cannot imagine the agony I go through when I think of you facing men like that Billy Ringo and that . . . that other man at the Heaston place. Suppose it had been a gun Ringo was reaching for and you hadn't been watching for such a trick?"

"You believed me when I said he reached inside his coat for a hidden gun?"

"Of course," she replied. Her brow knitted into a frown.

"And the shooting at the Heaston's? It was *because* of Callie Heaston, not over her like some have said. I was doing only what any lawman, sworn to protect the people under his authority, would do. You believe that, too?"

She looked at him. "I have always believed in you and the things you have to do. Just because there was a woman involved, why should it be any different?"

He made no reply but drew her quickly to his chest and kissed

83

her fully on the lips. She would never know how much her saying those words meant to him. She trusted him, believed in
him. Nothing else mattered. Not Cameo Crossing, not Walker
Rohle, not anything. They would go away just as she wished. If
she didn't want him to be a lawman, that was the way it would
be. He could punch cattle, maybe get a job as a foreman on
some ranch. Or perhaps they might manage to get their hands
on a small spread somewhere and start building it up. It didn't
really matter. The important thing was they would be together
for all time with nothing of the past standing between them.

"When can you be ready to leave?" he asked, releasing her
from his arms.

"Whenever you say."

"In the morning, then. I've a few things that must be done.
Find Humboldt and draw what money I've got stashed away.
And make a deal with Kane for a buggy."

She was at once serious. "Mark, I hope you won't oppose me
in this. I know how you feel about my father but I would like
him to marry us. Is it all right?"

Nothing mattered, now that all things were settled. He said:
"Sure. But my guess is that he will refuse. He ordered me to
stay away from you. He's not going to like what you're doing."

"I know," she murmured. "I heard him and what you said."
She smiled. "If he won't, there are plenty other ministers. But I
would like to ask him. I think he will agree when he sees I have
made up my mind."

"Will that be tonight?"

"In the morning, just before we leave."

"Do you want me to tell him, that we are going to marry, I
mean?"

She shook her dark head. "No, it's something I want to do
myself. I think it will be better."

Kennicott drew her close for another kiss, and they turned

for the doorway. All his worries, all his bothersome troubles had fled, resolving themselves in those last few minutes. The problems of Cameo Crossing would soon be far behind him with a bright and shining future with Judith opening up ahead.

They entered the street, busy now with dusk's traffic. A half a dozen or more wagons and buggies were spotted along the way, their owners doing business now that coolness had come. Three cowboys jogged in from the east, lifting their hands in greeting as they passed. Somewhere a dog was barking and the steady pound of the blacksmith upon iron at Leo Kane's was a continuing ring in the stagnant air.

"It's a nice little town," Judith murmured wistfully. "I sort of hate leaving it."

Kennicott ducked his head. "Too bad it has to die," he said in a tight voice.

She glanced up to him, curious at his words, at his tone. His eyes had lifted sharply, watching something down the street. There was a small group of people, among them Clete McCoy and Tom Girard, the squat, gray-haired editor of the local weekly newspaper, gathered in front of the Trail Queen.

As they watched, Girard's wife laid her hand upon her husband's shoulder and attempted to draw him away. Girard stood his ground stubbornly, voicing some statement or other with a vigorous nodding of his head. In that next moment Mc-Coy took a long step forward, grasped the little newspaperman by the shirt front with his left hand, and smashed a fist into his face.

Girard's head wobbled from the blow. Again McCoy struck him and the older man's knees buckled. He tried to fight back, flailing out weakly with his clenched hands but to no avail. Girard's wife then tried to pull her husband free, but McCoy sent her sprawling into the dust with a shove.

"Seems the news has already got around," Kennicott said

through compressed lips. He started down the street at once for the Trail Queen. Without turning he said to Judith: "Better you go home."

Judith said—"No."—in a short, quick way and hurried to keep pace with his long strides.

XI

The crowd around McCoy and the Girards had increased considerably by the time Kennicott and Judith Lockridge arrived. All were silent, making no effort to intervene, maintaining a safe and respectable distance. Like most gatherings in such circumstances they were shocked, sickened by the brutality of the uneven match. But they feared to lift a hand to halt it.

Kennicott pushed roughly through the circle. Girard was sitting on the ground, his shoddy gray suit marked with dust and blood that dripped steadily from his large, thickly veined nose. His wife had regained her feet and was brushing futilely at her black satin dress, sobbing raggedly.

"Next time you got a mind to say something about me in that two-bit paper of yours be damn' sure it's something good," McCoy was saying.

Kennicott rushed in. He hit the man hard on the point of his chin. McCoy went stumbling backward and fell full length. The lawman was after him, almost before he struck. He grasped the gunman by the shirt front and dragged him to an upright position.

"I've had about enough of you for one day," he said, and slapped McCoy across his scarred face.

McCoy lifted his hands to ward off any further blows, trying all the while to tear loose from Kennicott's vise-like grip. A voice in the crowd, now brave, said: "Give it to him, Marshal!"

Kennicott released his grip. McCoy fell back a step, breathing deeply. A smear of blood lay at one corner of his mouth where the lawman's slashing hand had crushed his thin lips.

"You ain't got the right," he said, his face livid with anger. "You ain't the marshal around here now. I'll kill you for this. You wait."

"Maybe," Kennicott said. "As for not being the marshal, I'm not through yet."

His cold glance flicked down to the gun at McCoy's hip. "This is the second time I've caught you wearing a gun today. You know the law around here." He moved up to McCoy and jerked the heavy gun from its holster.

"Walker Rohle told me to wear that gun . . . ," McCoy said.

"Walker Rohle's not running this town . . . not yet," Kennicott said.

Thrusting the pistol into his belt, he turned and, bending down, helped Tom Girard to his feet. The old man was still somewhat dazed from the attack.

"I'm not forgetting this, Kennicott," McCoy said.

Mark ignored the half threat. "What's this all about, Tom?"

Girard shook his head. "Reckon he didn't like something I said about him in my paper. It was a month ago."

Kennicott considered that for a moment. He swiveled his attention back to McCoy. "You're a little slow in bringing up the matter, Clete. Any special reason for the delay?"

McCoy made no reply. He simply stared at Kennicott, his twisted face red and angry.

"Maybe for the reason that you'd heard this town no longer had a marshal. That I was finished here and you and your kind could go back to the old way."

McCoy said nothing. A woman in the crowd asked, in a faint, faltering voice: "Is that true, Marshal? You've resigned?"

"By request," Kennicott replied over his shoulder. To McCoy he added: "Get off the street, Clete. Stay out of my sight until I'm gone. If I catch you once more trying to pull anything, I'll give you a chance to use a gun."

"Like you did Billy Ringo?" McCoy said.

"Like Billy Ringo," Kennicott said.

McCoy's eyes showed their surprise at the answer. He evidently had not expected Kennicott to answer in such a way. His gaze locked with that of the lawman for a moment, and then, retrieving his hat, he wheeled and started for the Trail Queen.

Kennicott watched him go in thoughtful silence. He was seeing not only the swaggering, bullying form of Clete McCoy but all of the McCoys of different names who would soon descend upon Cameo Crossing, that would be walking its streets and frequenting its buildings and shoving the Tom Girards around. That would be the way of things—the Clete McCoys ruling the town, running roughshod, having their tough and brutal time.

His eyes came back to the Girards. Judith was helping the editor's wife straighten up her disarranged clothing. Now that the excitement was over, most of the crowd had drifted away.

"My thanks, Marshal," Girard mumbled, rubbing at his chin. "There was a time when I'd have needed no help for the likes of Clete McCoy. But I reckon that's gone. Years sure have a way of slipping up on a man."

"I don't figure he'll bother you any more," Kennicott said. But his words sounded hollow and meaningless in his ears.

Girard looked at him speculatively. "Is it true . . . what I heard about you resigning?"

Kennicott nodded. "By request, like I said. I'm the wrong kind of lawman for this town, it seems."

"I doubt if that's everybody's opinion," Girard stated flatly. "I was coming to talk to you about it when McCoy stopped me."

"Well, it's what the men who are running this town seem to think. If you have any objections, tell it to them. Get a few people together and complain about it."

Girard shook his head. "You know that couldn't be done, Mark. People around here, the majority anyway, won't stand up to Rohle and the merchants. They can't afford to. They've got families to feed." The editor paused. His lined face became intent. "I hate to see you walk out on us right now. You're all we've got standing between us and another Hell Street. You just saw a sample of what it will be like."

Kennicott felt Judith's hand, warm and assuring, slip into his own, making him more aware of her presence and reminding him of their plans for the future.

She said: "Mark has made up his mind, Mister Girard. He has resigned and we're getting married. We're leaving in the morning."

Girard's eyes opened in surprise; he was plainly startled by the news. He recovered and murmured: "My best to you both. Well, if you've made up your mind, there's no use talking about it. Lots of people will hate to see you go, Mark."

"You'll have another marshal," Kennicott said. "He'll keep things straight."

"A man appointed by Walker Rohle? Don't be a fool, Mark. It wouldn't surprise me one bit if McCoy isn't wearing your badge the minute you've pulled out."

Kennicott mulled that prediction through his head. His glance was lost in the faint haze of hills in the west, turning deep purple now with the setting of the sun. "I hate to think it would be McCoy," he said, half aloud.

"McCoy or any one of Rohle's bunch . . . what difference would it make? It'll all turn out the same. Decent men or women won't have a chance. They'll never know a minute's peace and safety."

Kennicott felt Judith's fingers tighten upon his own.

He was thinking of Cameo Crossing, of what it was and what it would be like if it fell into the clutches of a lawman such as

Clete McCoy would be. Backed by Rohle they could, and would, try anything. But it was no skin off his back, he suddenly assured himself, shrugging off the thought. The town would likely live through it. The Tom Girards might even grow a little backbone if they finally had to stand up and fight a little for their rights. But it was a hard thing to do, just to turn away, knowing what they were in for. A little like leaving a suffering animal in a trap when you might do something about it.

Judith said: "We've a lot to do, Mark. Hadn't we better start?" There was a trace of anxiety in her tone, as if she had become fearful of the moments and what might lie within them.

Girard smiled wanly at the girl. "I'm sorry, Miss Lockridge, but I've got to say this. I know you want Mark to quit, to leave, but there's everything at stake here for most of us. I'm begging you, Mark, for the sake of the people in this town, don't walk out on us now. Maybe they haven't the courage to ask it of you, but I have. I know what will happen around here."

Kennicott turned to Judith. She was looking up at him appealingly, hoping for the best, aware of the struggle that was tearing at him and praying it would resolve itself soon and rightly. But she would say nothing either way; it must be his own decision. She would say no more to influence him.

"If you'd just stay for a short time. Until I could get a few people worked up or until we could find a marshal we could trust. That's all I'm asking."

If he did, it could possibly mean the finish for all the plans he and Judith had made. Kennicott realized that. The fight would be sharp and bitter and her father would be deeply involved with the opposing faction. Anything could happen. But it shouldn't be something that would come between them. Nothing could ever change the way he felt about Judith, and, if she loved him, a few more days wouldn't mean anything. It, in reality, was a trivial thing when you considered they had a lifetime awaiting them.

"I don't think it would hurt to stick around a few days longer," he said, turning to her. "At least until we're sure everything is all right."

Girard's face lit up with new hope. Kennicott felt Judith's hand slip away from his. She turned her eyes, looking away, her features stilled and without expression. He would feel better about the whole thing; he wouldn't be leaving with a feeling of guilt in his mind.

"What do you think, Judith?" he asked. "Would it be all right?"

Without moving she said: "If we don't leave in the morning, Mark, we'll never leave."

Kennicott started to reply when a commotion at the swinging doors of the Trail Queen drew him back. Alf Wisdom and Pete Cable, a man who, during his sober moments, did the town's sign painting, came out onto the porch. They were carrying between them a large, canvas banner. They strung it across the front window of the saloon, tacking it into place with much hammering, and then stepped back to view their handiwork.

WELCOME OX!

The bold, black letters flung their message in Kennicott's face. The bars were really down! The merchants had invited King Overmeyer and his wild bunch to Cameo Crossing. In the next instant Kennicott realized something more; that invitation had been extended days ago, long before the matter of his resignation had come up. Walker Rohle and the others had been that sure of themselves and their power.

"Lord help us," Mrs. Girard said.

"They'll sure wreck this town," Girard said. "After what you did to them when you drove them out, they'll make up for it now."

Kennicott was silent for a full minute. He shook his head.

91

"No, not this time, Tom," he said slowly. "Now, I'll have to stick around. I can't leave with them coming in."

He heard Girard murmur—"Thank heaven."—and turned then to look at Judith, to explain, if necessary, the need for his remaining. She had moved away from him and was walking sadly toward the parsonage.

XII

Kennicott started to follow the girl, to overtake her and attempt to make her understand. She must realize the obligation he felt, the duty he must honor or else he would spend the rest of a lifetime with that scar of having failed the town when it needed him most lying bright and accusingly across his conscience. But then some of his masculine hard pride stayed him. He would not beg.

Hands clawed at his arms, at his shoulders. Someone slapped him on the back. Tom Girard's voice said: "Mark, I knew you wouldn't desert us. We can sleep easy this night."

You can, Kennicott thought bitterly, *but how about me? What about my life? What about the things I'd like to do and the plans I have?*

Almost roughly he shook free of the detaining fingers. He was thinking like a fool, like a spoiled kid not getting his way. He was a lawman first, last, and all the way down the line, sworn to protect the weak and the helpless. To these his personal interests were secondary. But try as he would he could not pull his gaze from Judith. It was like a dream walking out on him.

"What's going on here?" Jim Dry asked above the murmur of the group. "What's this all about, Tom?"

Girard, with obvious satisfaction, said: "Something you won't be pleased to hear."

"Meaning?"

Kennicott, mad all the way through, whirled. "He means

there's been a little slip-up in your plans." It was the Jim Drys that caused things like losing Judith, like losing the town to happen to him. "He means that plan of yours hit a snag. I'm not handing over my badge. I'm sticking around until Overmeyer and his bunch get here and I'll take care of them when they arrive."

Dry's eyes widened in surprise. He looked blank for a moment, and then a sly smile crossed his weathered face. "Guess again, Marshal. You don't have no choice. You either resign or we suspend you. You'll have no authority."

"Maybe not," Kennicott replied coolly. "But I'm still wearing the gun and the badge. And I know what's right and wrong even if the rest of you seem to have forgotten."

"We represent the merchants of this town," Dry said. "And the people."

"You represent yourselves." Kennicott's voice was hard and flat. "Maybe a few others might string along because they're afraid not to. I don't know and I sure don't care. But there's one thing you can get straight in your head and trot over to Rohle and tell . . . I'm not resigning. I'm right here until this mess is cleared up, right here, in fact, until the mayor gets back and appoints a new marshal, if need be."

"We'll see about that," Dry said. "I think you'll find out mighty quick who runs this town. And we don't let nobody tell us what we can do."

"Well, I'm telling you this," Kennicott answered, "I won't resign. That's the way it stands. Now, you better run along and tell that to Rohle. And to Mister Lockridge," he added as an afterthought.

Dry stared at him for a long, quiet moment. Then: "I'll tell them all right. Both of them. But you're bucking the wrong herd, Marshal. You'll find that out quick enough."

Kennicott shrugged. "One thing more you'd better tell Rohle.

Tell him to get word to Overmeyer to stay out of town. It's still closed to him and his OX bunch."

He moved off then, not waiting for any further words from the merchant. Tom Girard halted him once again with a hand laid upon his shoulder.

"Mark, if I . . . we've upset your plans, with Judith, I mean, I'm right sorry. Maybe when Overmeyer hears you're not leaving, he'll swing clear of the town. Then you could maybe go ahead with what you had in mind."

Kennicott shook his head. "He's not likely to do that. Not after he's been invited. And you're forgetting one thing."

"Oh? What's that?"

"He's got a lot of extra backbone nowadays. He's got Dave Seringo working for him. That's his new trump card and he won't be backing down for anybody, not with Seringo to do his fighting for him."

"Seringo," Girard said, "that's bad, real bad. Guess things are even worse than I figured. Looks like we really talked you into a pot of trouble this time, Mark."

Kennicott grinned wryly. "You didn't talk me into anything, Tom. I'd say it was that sign Rohle nailed up that made up my mind for me. Could be, if he'd waited another day, until I was over the hill. . . ."

He started on then, not finishing what he intended to say. A voice reached after him: "Anyway, Marshal, we appreciate your staying around and we're thanking you for it." He nodded but he did not stop.

"Mark!"

He turned at the sound of Alberta Heaston's call. She was standing before Jergenson's, invitation in her eyes. "Come in and have a cup of coffee."

He said: "Thanks, no. Think I'll pass it up until later."

The tall, lank form of a man moved in behind her, coming

from inside the café. He pushed by the girl and stepped into the open. It was Curly Dan Sprewl. Kennicott stiffened.

"Come ahead, Marshal," the gunman drawled. "Ain't polite, turnin' down a lady's invite."

Sprewl halted at the edge of the boardwalk. He returned Kennicott's gaze insolently, glancing down to his own waist.

"No need lookin' for a gun, Marshal. I checked mine with the bartender, just like the law said to do."

"What do you want here?" Kennicott asked.

"Why, nothin', purely nothin'. Just figured I'd lay over in this town for a spell. Real nice place, Marshal."

"There's plenty others," Kennicott said. "You start traveling to one of them by morning. I don't want you hanging around here."

"Now, wait just a minute, Marshal. You can't do that. I ain't breakin' no laws and I got a right to stay here if I want to. Seems to me that's what's got you in trouble now . . . runnin' people around to suit yourself."

"You be gone by morning," Kennicott said coldly. "Don't worry any about me."

Sprewl gave Kennicott a dry grin and strolled out into the street, heading for the Trail Queen. Alberta started to say something, but hesitated as Jergenson, his huge shape filling the doorway, came into view.

"That's a bad thing, Marshal," the café man said in his thick accent, "my customer driving off in such way. He was only supper eating."

"He ever eat there before?" Kennicott asked.

"He is new business," Jergenson answered.

"And he'll be gone tomorrow, most likely." He turned to Alberta. "He was one of the men at your ma's place this morning. It was his brother I had to shoot."

Alberta's eyes widened. "Then . . . he's here to get even with you for that."

Ray Hogan

Kennicott shrugged. "He'll have to get in line with the rest of them," he said, and went on down the street.

XIII

Jeff Wallis was pretty much a creature of habit. He arose at the same time each morning, following an identical routine in his preparation for the day. Precisely at 6:45 A.M. he arrived at Jergenson's Café. There he would have eggs, meat, fried potatoes, and drink two cups of coffee. This done, he would leave the café and walk down the center of the street to the jail. It was accomplished with such unvarying exactitude that many along the way vowed a man could set his timepiece by the old deputy's movements.

It was no particular compliment. It reflected instead the pattern of his existence. He had come into Cameo Crossing after Kennicott's deadly accurate guns had tamed it of its lawlessness and assumed the combination job of jailer and deputy at a time when the most desperate character to be found in town would be an overly enthusiastic cowpuncher, celebrating pay day with too much red-eye.

Prior to that, before the argument Between the States broke out, he had been a clerk in an Eastern dry goods firm. He enlisted in the Army, hoping for escape from a dust-dry existence, and was promptly relegated to the ranks of the paper brigade. He spent the entire conflict doing menial office work for lower grade officers. Thus his life continued to be one of colorless years, a history of a man never quite reaching a goal, of never performing anything of consequence or accomplishing anything of value. He was destined to be one of those faceless millions who are born, live, and die without being noticed. When the war was over, he drifted West with the tide, cut free from old times and old ways by the devastation.

Eventually he found himself broke and hungry in Cameo Crossing. Kennicott befriended him and, soon after, needing a deputy, gave him his chance.

Now, sitting there at the table in Jergenson's, his supper only half eaten, he listened to the words of Keith Crandall while a warm glow began to build thickly within him.

"Understand this, Jeff," the merchant said, leaning forward in a confidential manner, "there's nothing official about this yet. But you can pretty well bank on it. Mark Kennicott's quit and you're the only man to fill his job."

Wallis, a man forever familiar to the wrong turn of cards and no stranger to disappointment, permitted himself the luxury of a moment's thrilling dream. Town marshal. And of an important place like Cameo Crossing. It was unbelievable—none of the positions, none of the heights he had aspired to in the far-distant past could compare with this. He envisioned himself doing the job, wearing a new hat, a white one perhaps; there would be new boots with fancy, colored-thread stitching. And a pair of those black, whipcord britches cut close to fit the legs. Maybe he should have a new gun, too. He was still using one Kennicott had taken off a drifter who later got himself killed in a saloon.

The ancient caution, born of heartache, moved in. He shook his head vigorously, clearing away such thoughts.

Hell, he didn't even have the job yet. And you couldn't go much by Crandall. He liked to play the big man and shoot off his mouth. He lifted his gaze to the merchant. There was a strain of doubt lacing in with a fine thread of hope in his voice when he spoke. "You sure Kennicott's leaving?"

Crandall nodded. "For dead certain. You can forget about him. He's finished here."

Wallis mulled that about. "Maybe I'm too old for the job," he offered doubtfully.

"Too old! What do you mean, too old? We don't need any

young bucko around here any more. Town's quiet. It's been tamed. All we need is a man with a cool head on his shoulders and experience under his hat. Hell, all he has to do is stand around and look like a lawman. Let everybody see we got a marshal, that's all."

"Ain't had much experience, except what I got here under Kennicott."

"That's enough. And you got it right here in Cameo. That's good, too. You know this town and everybody knows you."

"The others . . . you figure they'll let me have it?"

Crandall said: "I'm sure. And I'll see to it that you get it. The committee will be looking for recommendations. I'll stand for you. And Kane and a couple more I know will back me." He paused, studying the older man intently with half-shut eyes.

"You tell them I'll sure do a good job for them. They won't need to worry none. And I'll appreciate it no end."

"Only right you should have it," the merchant said with a wave of his hand. "You're the logical man. Anyway, I figure old friends like you and me ought to work together. Sort of look out for each other, that right, Jeff?"

Wallis nodded slowly, apparently having some thoughts on the subject. Finally he said: "Now, I sure want nothing to do with this unless Kennicott's quitting. I don't want him thinking I'm after his job."

"Kennicott resigned over there in the parson's parlor a couple hours ago. Rohle and the parson are writing out a paper for him to sign so it will be all legal and such. Don't worry about him. You won't be taking his job. You'll just be filling the vacancy left by him going. Why, if you don't take it, we'll have to hire somebody else. A stranger, most likely."

"Then I reckon that settles it. If they want me, I'd sure admire having the job."

Crandall pushed back from the table. "There'll probably be a meeting tonight in Rohle's place to handle it. It might be a good idea for you to be handy."

Wallis nodded. "I'll be downstairs. I might sit in on a hand or two of cards, sort of celebrating, you could say."

"Good enough," Crandall said, and started for the doorway.

"Sure appreciate this, Keith," Wallis called after him, "your backing me, I mean."

"Forget it, Jeff," the merchant replied with a wide smile. "What's a man got friends for if they ain't to give him a boost when they can?"

He passed on into the street, and for a time Wallis stared at the empty space that had framed the merchant's figure. He was thinking, not of what the man had last said but of the honor and glory suddenly coming his way at long last. Finally, after a lifetime of mediocrity, he was to become a man of importance; someone who would be looked up to and respected. Even feared, for the badge of authority carried its own weight most of the time. And he would live up to his responsibilities, they need not worry about that. He would not fail them or their trust in him. He would do a good job of keeping the town orderly and quiet, just like Kennicott had done.

He paused in his musing—the question—*why did Mark Kennicott resign?*—presenting itself. Was it over this argument about opening up the town again? Probably. Well, there must be an answer to that problem somewhere. It wasn't necessary to be bull-headed about such things and Kennicott often was blind to the other side of an argument. One thing he had learned many years ago was that you couldn't fight the powers that be, the Rohles and the Lockridges, those who run things. Best to work out a way to get along with them. Of course, Kennicott was right about not wanting to open the town up, but there must be some way it could be handled so everybody would end up satisfied.

Yet it would be kind of hard to see Kennicott leave. He was a good man; actually you might say he was Cameo Crossing itself. And he was about the finest man Wallis had ever met, bar none. He owed him a lot for taking him in that day and later on giving him a job. In so doing he had been directly responsible for putting him in place to inherit the marshal's star. Yes, he owed a lot to Mark Kennicott.

He became vaguely aware of the waitress, Alberta Heaston, standing at his table. "You want something else, Mister Wallis? More coffee maybe?"

The deputy nodded. A third cup was unusual for him but this was an unusual moment. She completed the refilling and turned back for the kitchen, carrying the granite pot with both hands. She was a real nice girl, Alberta was. Like her mother. Maybe, after he got started on the new job, he would pay a few calls on Callie Heaston. She was a mighty fine-looking woman and he had always admired her. From a distance, of course, as a deputy's wages and standing didn't leave much room for plans of marriage. But after he was town marshal that would change. He could afford a wife then. And a town marshal ought to be married.

He finished off his coffee and got slowly to his feet. Picking his hat off the chair back upon which he had hung it, he walked to the door. He did not enter the street but doubled back along the alley that ran along the rear of the buildings on the east side. An idea had come to him. He would go see Leo Kane and talk to him about the marshal's job, ask him to stand for him when the committee met. Crandall would do all he said he would, but a man shouldn't leave anything to chance. He should take a few measures on his own behalf himself. That's the way men who got places did it.

Then he would see Kennicott and tell him how things were shaping up, that he was to be his successor. Kennicott would be pleased to hear it, he was certain.

XIV

From the vantage point of his upstairs windows Walker Rohle had watched the encounter between Kennicott and Clete Mc-Coy. He could not distinctly hear what was being said but it took no imagination to realize matters were at harsh stages between his man and the tall marshal. Moments later he heard hammering in front of the Trail Queen, directly beneath, and knew the sign he had directed Cable to paint was being installed. As he watched Kennicott read it, he frowned, slightly irritated.

He should have told Alf Wisdom to wait until morning before hanging the banner welcoming King Overmeyer and his crew. Doing it this way was a little like waving a flag in a longhorn steer's eyes. Things would have gone off some smoother if they had possessed the presence of mind to wait until Kennicott was out of sight.

But on the other hand it didn't matter much. What could Mark Kennicott do about it? A half smile curved Rohle's lips. In a way, it was a form of tribute to him, to his power. Alf showed by this prompt and immediate action that he considered Rohle the supreme and ultimate word in the town; he was not worrying about any probable repercussions from the marshal or anyone else.

He watched idly as Judith wheeled abruptly and walked away from Kennicott, her shoulders stiff and square, her head tilted at an angry angle. He had a moment's wonder as to what had passed between them for, whatever it was, they were in strong disagreement and this, too, pleased him greatly.

Jim Dry moved into his vision. He saw him push his way into the cluster of people below and start a conversation with Tom Girard and Kennicott. Dry had a surprised look on his face while Kennicott spoke, surprised and disturbed. That was the trouble with small men like Dry. They let the little things upset

101

them. The merchant talked with the lawman for a few moments, and then wheeled toward the doors of the Trail Queen. Whatever it was all about, he would soon know. Dry was trotting up to tell him.

He waited until the knock came upon the door, and then crossed the room casually to slip the lock. It was a habit he had acquired somewhere back in the forgotten past always to keep a locked door behind himself. When he left his quarters, even if for only moments, he turned the lock. And when once again inside, the door remained secure. It was one of those unexplainable idiosyncrasies a man assumed somewhere along the road, never knowing exactly when or where but which stick with him all the rest of his days. And oft times prove the undoing of him.

Clete McCoy was with Dry, looking hot and angry with deep crimson color lying on the sides of his face. Kennicott's open palm had punished him severely. Rohle let the pair in and motioned them to the couch.

"What was all that about?"

Dry waved his hands in disgust. "This damn' fool," he exclaimed, ducking his head at McCoy, "had to go and pick a fight with Kennicott! He's upset the whole deal."

"I never picked no fight with him," McCoy denied hotly. "He horned in on somethin' that wasn't his business."

"And Alf . . . nailing up that danged sign right in front of Kennicott's eyes. Why didn't he have sense enough to wait till morning? At least until dark."

Rohle circled his ornate desk and sat down. His features were still, his eyes deeply thoughtful. "What do you mean . . . upset the whole deal?"

"Kennicott's changed his mind about resigning. Said to tell you so. Said you'd better warn Overmeyer to stay out of town."

Rohle studied the heavy ring on his finger. After a moment he began to twist it, around and around in that nervous way of his, causing the diamond to emit small, bright flashes when it caught light from the lamp on the desk.

He shook his head. "Well, what's done is done. It's unfortunate that things like this have to occur. They just create new problems. But I think it's not so bad."

"You mean Kennicott's not resigning ain't so bad?" Dry demanded.

Rohle lifted his shoulders and let them fall. "It would have been easier if he had, but, since he has changed his mind, that finishes that thought. I don't see that we need to worry over it, however."

"But if he won't quit, he stays on as marshal. Then what?"

"We'll go right ahead as we planned. We suspend him. And a marshal without authority has no power."

"There are a few people around here, quite a few maybe, who ain't going to like that. They'll agree with Kennicott."

"Let them," Rohle said easily. "What difference will it make? You think they'll stand up and fight for him?"

Dry wagged his head. "Maybe not. But you know Kennicott. He's not going to just stand by and watch King and his boys ride into town and not do anything about it."

"One thing you're forgetting, Jim . . . the last time the marshal ran King out, Dave Seringo wasn't working for him."

"Seringo," the merchant echoed. "By Judas, that's right."

"And I don't think Dave will take kindly to anyone, marshal or not, telling him what he can or can't do."

"That's a sure-fire cinch," McCoy agreed, his admiration for the gunman strongly evident in his tone.

"Then you figure all we've got to do is stand by and wait?" Dry asked.

"It's that simple," Rohle said. "Kennicott will have no authority as marshal, therefore he'll be acting on his own. I don't think we need to mention anything, one way or another to

Seringo. Just let him handle it."

"You think Seringo can stand up to Kennicott in a showdown? The marshal's a mighty good man with a pistol."

"He ain't as fast as Seringo," McCoy said. "I'd bet my last dollar on that."

Dry ignored McCoy, waiting for Rohle to express his opinion.

The saloonman said: "The marshal's good, no denying that. But maybe he's a bit out of practice. It's been some time since he stood up before a good gunman. I'll put my stack on Seringo, too."

"Then I reckon we've got nothing to worry over," Dry said with a long sigh. "We'll just leave things ride along and let nature take its course, eh?"

"Exactly," Rohle said. He arose and the two men followed quickly. They crossed the room and Rohle let them out onto the balcony overlooking the floor below. "I'll see you later," he said, dismissing the merchant, but to Clete McCoy he crooked a finger.

"One thing I want you to do," he said when the scar-faced man had come back to the doorway. "Seringo will have his hands full with Kennicott. No use fooling ourselves about that. Your job will be to keep Jeff Wallis out of the way if things come to a showdown. Understand?"

McCoy nodded. "Sure. I understand."

"But only if it comes to a showdown," Rohle repeated. "That straight, too?"

Again McCoy nodded. "I got it straight," he said, and moved back again across the balcony.

It was full dark when Jeff Wallis reached the jail and turned into its darkened interior. Kennicott had not yet struck a light to one of the lamps. Wallis could see his long frame slumped in a chair before his desk.

"You afraid of bushwhackers?" he asked in high good humor as he dragged a match across his seat.

Kennicott stirred, the chair setting up a loud squeak under his weight. "Just never noticed it was dark."

Wallis removed the chimney from a lamp, touched the wick with the burning match, and, when the flame had caught, carefully replaced the glass. He stationed the lamp in one of the wall brackets and faced Kennicott.

"Ran into Keith Crandall down at Jergenson's when I was eating supper. Right sorry to hear what happened."

"Bound to come sooner or later," the lawman replied absently.

"One thing I want you to know, Mark. I sure do appreciate all the things you've done for me. Giving me a job as your deputy and such."

Kennicott's glance swung inquiringly to the older man's seamy face. "I needed a man and you were looking for a job. That made it right for both of us. And you've done a good job as deputy. I'm grateful and I've got no complaints."

"Much obliged," Wallis said in a muffled voice. "One thing I want you to know is that things will be run just the same around here. I don't figure to let anybody do any changing that ain't right. I'll keep this town straight."

"You'll keep it straight?" Kennicott said. "What's all this about, Jeff?"

"Crandall told me about your resigning. They're going to put me in your place. I'll be taking over soon as you turn in your star."

Kennicott stiffened in his chair. "Crandall told you all this?"

"Just a few minutes ago. While I was having supper at Jergenson's. You know what, Mark?" he added, his voice filled with youthfulness, "I'll be making more money on the job. Figure I might jump off and take myself a wife. Thinking about Callie Heaston. You reckon she'd be interested?"

Kennicott removed his legs from the desk, planted his feet on the floor, and got up slowly. He moved over to the doorway. Cameo Crossing was a lengthy shadow now, outlined against the night sky with yellow squares of lamplit windows interspersed. The piano at the Trail Queen was tinkling in a tinny, discordant way and somewhere, farther along the street, a mother was calling her tardy child in for its evening meal.

He listened for a time, and then said: "That's all fine, Jeff. I know you would do a good job. But there's one thing wrong with it."

"Wrong? How so?"

"I'm not resigning," Kennicott said, softening his voice as best he could. "At least not now. Maybe not ever."

Breath ran out of Jeff Wallis in a slow, exhausted sigh. He seemed to shrink, to grow smaller and older until he was no more than a thin, half-bent line in the gloom.

"Might have figured it," he murmured, expressing in those few words the disappointment of every man interminably defeated by the quirks of fate. "Appears Crandall didn't know what he was talking about."

"He didn't have it all wrong," Kennicott said. "I first told them I was quitting. That was the way they wanted it. Then a couple of things happened that changed my mind. Didn't you see that sign they nailed up in front of Rohle's place?"

Wallis shook his head. "Didn't come up the street. Was down talking to Leo Kane and come by the alley."

"They hung it late this afternoon. They've already invited Overmeyer back."

Jeff Wallis made no reply. Ordinarily it would have evoked an explosion of pointed opinion pertaining to the stupidity of certain people. Now, he stood silent in the hush of the small office; he was thinking of what might have been, of the glory that was almost within his grasp.

Nothing ever changes, the bitter words raced across his mind, *always something happens when I'm about to be favored. Seems where other men turn up aces, I draw the deuce.*

"You know what that means for us . . . Overmeyer and his crew coming into town," Kennicott was saying. "Trouble and plenty of it. And Sprewl's brother's in town, gunning for me or I miss my guess. I told him to be gone by morning but I doubt if he listens."

Wallis shrugged and turned to the lamp. Cupping his hand behind the smoked chimney, he turned down the wick and blew out the flame. Like his own bright hopes, he thought, whisked into blackness.

"I reckon we can handle them," he said, moving toward the door. " 'Night. See you in the morning."

Kennicott made his reply and Wallis walked out into the street, his boot heels dragging a bit on the sun-baked earth. The noise from the Trail Queen was much louder, more pronounced, and that drew his momentary attention. But it was not trouble, he soon decided, only people having their good time, celebrating. That brought to mind his own intentions for the evening.

He swung sharply to the opposite direction, heading for the old, shabby clapboard dwelling where he maintained a single room. There was no need for celebration now.

XV

It was near noon. 11:00 A.M. to be exact.

Jeff Wallis, standing in the doorway of the jail, said to Kennicott: "Here they come. Part of them, anyway."

Kennicott arose, checked the loads in his pistol. He reached for the short-barreled shotgun standing in the corner rack, broke it open, and assured himself its two chambers were filled. That done, he moved out into the bright sunlight.

There were seven riders in the group, only a small part of King Overmeyer's considerable trail crew. The advance guard, the lawman thought. They rode arrogantly abreast, spreading across the road's entire width. When they reached the beginning of the street at the town's limit, the phalanx did not break but came steadily on, disregarding pedestrians and vehicles alike with a fine contempt.

They swung past the jail. One of the riders, his brown face toward the lawmen, smirked broadly. "Looky there, boys! You-all best be on your Sunday school manners, else them fierce-lookin' peace officers will put you in their pokey!"

The man riding slightly in the lead was not King Overmeyer. He was Dave Seringo, a husky, hard-featured man with empty eyes, colorless as rain. He wore a dark, shabby suit and a dirty red and white striped silk shirt that stood out with startling clarity. Instead of the usual wide-brimmed cattle country headgear, he had on a small, black felt hat now well covered with trail dust. He was not listening to his fellow rider's comments; at that moment his glance was upon Judith Lockridge, standing on the parsonage porch.

After the OX rider had spoken, he swung his indolent gaze to Kennicott and the deputy. He muttered something to his companions, inaudible to the marshal and Wallis. It evoked a loud laugh from the OX crew members.

Kennicott watched them pass on down the suddenly deserted street without comment. He waited until they had pulled up to the hitching bar in front of the Trail Queen and then, without turning, said to Wallis: "Let's go."

"We running them out?" the deputy asked.

"Got a better idea," Kennicott said. "Rohle is so anxious to have them around, we'll just take their guns and keep them corralled in his place until the rest come. Any damage done it will be done to the Trail Queen."

Wallis grunted his appreciation for the plan. "You going to take Seringo's gun?"

"Seringo first of all," Kennicott said. "Any reason why I shouldn't?"

Wallis wagged his head. "Just wanted to know how to figure things."

The deputy fell in behind the marshal, saying no more. He had not again mentioned to Kennicott the matter of his resigning and the fact that he would have been wearing the marshal's star had not the big lawman changed his mind. He was much the same man outwardly as he had been before talking to Keith Crandall and dreaming his thoughts of glory. An endless procession of disappointments temper any man and teach him to accept the bitter cards that fate dealt in stoical silence.

"I'll handle Seringo," Kennicott said over his shoulder. "You ride herd on the rest."

Cameo Crossing had gone stone quiet when they walked up to the OX crew. It was as if the entire town were awaiting with bated breath those next few critical moments, hoping for the best but fearing the worst. A town lived or died in such times. And if Dave Seringo came out the better in this encounter with Mark Kennicott, there was no question in anyone's mind concerning the future of Cameo Crossing.

Seringo came slowly around as the marshal drifted in on his right side. Wallis took up a position on the broad porch fronting the Trail Queen where he could overlook the remaining cowpunchers and keep them constantly in his view. The gunman's face was stiff and expectant, his hollow eyes no more than slits as he dropped into an easy, relaxed stance. There was no talking, no laughing among the riders. There was only a breathless, heavily laden tension.

"Well, Marshal? You got something on your mind?"

Kennicott, the shotgun cradled in the crook of his right arm and pointing carelessly at the gunman's belly, said: "I have. There's a law in this town that says no man wears a gun inside its limits. You're wearing one. So's the rest of your crew."

"So?"

"Either shuck them or keep on riding. Don't matter to me which."

A hard-cornered grin cracked Seringo's thin features. "Maybe we got some ideas about that. Maybe we figure to stick around a spell and keep the artillery, too."

"Either drop those gun belts or move on," Kennicott said. It was the same old battle, the lawless testing the law, running their bluff, seeing how far they might go. "I won't say it again, Seringo. Drop those guns or move on. And if you stay around, keep inside that saloon. I'll not have you, any of you, out on the street. I find you outside I'll throw you in a cell."

"You'll do all that?" Seringo said. "Now, that might be a right hard chore. Besides, take a look at that sign up there. Maybe you ain't read it yet. We got a invite to this town."

"The sign was no idea of mine," Kennicott snapped. "Now, what's it to be?"

Seringo returned the marshal's cool gaze, gradually lowering his own until it rested upon the twin muzzles of the shotgun pointed directly at him. But there was no uncertainty in his manner, no relenting to authority.

"You want my iron, Marshal, why, I reckon you'll just have to take it."

In the deadly, following hush Kennicott shifted the shotgun gently until it was only inches from Seringo's breast. With the thumb of his left hand he cocked the tall, rabbit-ear hammers, the sound popping loudly in the quiet. Saying nothing, he stepped forward and with a quick motion of his free hand, reached out and flipped Seringo's gun into the dust. The little gunman's eyes began to glow with a steady, hard brilliance and the line of his mouth tightened into a gray seam.

Not looking away from the man, Kennicott shouted: "Rest of you OX men! Drop your gun belts. Do it damned quick!"

There was an immediate, responding creak of leather followed by a series of solid thuds as the order was complied with.

"Collect them, Jeff," Kennicott said.

The deputy came off the porch and began picking up the abandoned belts and pistols.

"They'll be at the jail," Kennicott said. "You can have them when you ride out. Not before."

Wallis, the discarded belts looped over his left shoulder and arm, moved in to pick up Seringo's gun. In so doing he came in close to the wiry gunman. Kennicott, recognizing sudden threat, yelled: "Watch it, Jeff!"

In that same instant Seringo lunged against the deputy, knocking him hard into the side of the shotgun's barrels. It brushed the weapon away and set off both hammers. The twin charges of buckshot roared up into the sky harmlessly but it afforded Seringo the opportunity he sought. He snatched for the pistol lying in the street.

Kennicott let the shotgun fall. He threw himself at Seringo, his shoulder colliding with that of the man. It spun him slightly off balance and to one side. There was no time left in which to draw his own weapon. He swung his open hand down in a slashing blow at Seringo's head. The heel of it caught the gunman at the base of the neck and drove him full length, face down into the dust.

"Stand back!" Jeff Wallis said.

Kennicott angrily kicked Seringo's gun toward the deputy. Reaching down, he grasped the prostrate gunman by the collar and dragged him to his feet. Seringo, plastered with a liberal coat of Cameo Crossing's fine dust from toe to forehead, said nothing. He slowly brushed at his lips and face with the back of his hand.

"Best place for you is in jail," Kennicott said, not releasing his grip upon the gunman's coat.

Seringo's glance, brittle and hot, flicked the faces of the OX men. In slow, well-spaced words he said: "The day you do that, friend, is the day you better order your grave dug."

"Could be," Kennicott said. He had his gun out and now prodded Seringo savagely in the ribs. "Get moving. I've got other things to do." He added, throwing the words over his shoulder: "The rest of you, get inside that saloon and stay there. I don't want any of you on the street. That clear?"

There was a grumbling assent from the riders as they began to drift toward the swinging doors of the Trail Queen. Halfway across the porch they halted. Walker Rohle, followed by Jim Dry, Clete McCoy, and several other men, came into the open.

"One moment, Kennicott!"

Rohle's voice lashed across the stillness of the street, carrying to the watching, waiting citizens of the town. They had viewed the entire scene of the encounter with Seringo in breathless anticipation, not knowing just what to expect. Kennicott had won; now came a new threat, a duel of authority.

Kennicott jabbed the barrel of the pistol deeper into Seringo's back, causing the man to wince. "Hold it," he commanded softly. "And don't make any moves. Won't take much to make me pull this trigger."

Seringo came to a halt, and Kennicott circled about him until he faced Rohle and his group. "Well?"

Jim Dry spoke up at once. "You ain't the marshal no more, Kennicott. You can't put that man in jail."

"You watch me do it," the lawman said with no humor.

"On what charge?" Rohle spoke up then.

"Resisting the law. That will do for a start. I could think up a few more if necessary." He paused, throwing a hard, direct glance at the saloonman. "Why? You got some special interest in the matter?"

112

"Only one," Rohle said, looking about. "I don't like to see a visitor to our town pushed around. We've had too much of that already."

Kennicott laughed, a harsh, derisive sound that carried along the street. "First time I ever heard it put that way. This visitor, as you call him, is a known gunman. If he tries to use that pistol of his around here again, he'll get more than a pushing around."

"You've been susp- . . . ," Rohle began, but Seringo's level, lifeless voice cut him off.

"Don't lose any sleep over me, friend," he said, looking straight at Rohle. "I can skin my own snakes."

"King will see about this when he gets here!" one of the OX cowpunchers spoke up. "He'll take care of that tin-star marshal and his two-bit jail!"

Kennicott regarded the speaker sardonically. "Tell you what, cowboy," he said. "You make it easy for him. Tell him I'll be waiting at the jail to see him."

He swung back to Seringo. Ducking his head at the squat outline of the adobe structure at the end of the street, he said—"Move on."—and prodded the gunman again.

From the vine-shaded porch of the parsonage Judith and her father viewed the tense meeting. All during the breathless minutes when Kennicott first stepped up to Dave Seringo to the moment when he entered the jail with his prisoner, she had watched with a thudding apprehension in her heart.

"It is a surprise to me we did not witness another murder," George Lockridge said from behind her.

She whirled upon him. "That's not a fair thing to say!" she cried, her anxiety finding sudden release in a fierce defense of Kennicott. "Mark's strong and good . . . but you just won't see it."

"I see no good in any man that wantonly takes another's life," Lockridge replied stiffly. "Do you deny that he has done so?"

"Only because he had no other choice. It was his life or the other man's . . . and he was doing it in the line of duty. He can't be blamed for protecting himself."

Lockridge shook his head, his pale blue eyes appearing almost white in the strong sunlight. "That's where the problem lies, Judith," he said in a patient voice. "When is it necessary to defend one's life with a bullet? At what point of a conversation? I believe, as do many others, that Kennicott acted before it was necessary, that killing was uncalled for. Today was the exception, possibly because he knew the entire town was watching him."

Judith stared at her father's solemn, deeply grooved features. He was so sure of himself, of his convictions. There was no room in him for anything else, any doubts or misgivings that he could be wrong.

Tears flooded again into her eyes. "Oh, Papa! You just won't understand him or the things he must do. You only want to believe what you think is right . . . and make others believe the way you do. What Mark said about you is true . . . so true."

Lockridge moved closer to his daughter. He placed his huge hands upon her shoulders, awkwardly drawing her to him. They had never been very close, this father and daughter. Both had tried, possibly, but there was little mutual ground between them upon which they might trod.

"About me? What did he say about me?"

"That you are wrong in your thinking. That you will cause a lot of people to get hurt by saying the things you do when you really know nothing about it."

"I'm sure of one thing, as sure as I'm standing here. No man has the right to kill another. . . ."

"You think he likes to do that? You think he doesn't feel bad about it when it's over with . . . even when it's the worst, the lowest kind of man? Do you know it makes him sick . . . sick at heart and stomach when it's done with?"

Lockridge made no immediate reply. He watched her tear-stained face closely for a long minute. Then: "I thought you were forgetting him, Judith. I had hoped so. Now, again I find you defending him and his ways."

"I love him, Papa," she said simply. "And I am defending him because of what he has to do. I hope the time will come when he will find another way of life and yesterday I walked out on him because of it, because he felt he owed this town, you and all the other people in it, a debt of honor. I could not understand him then, but I think I do now. And I'm going back to him, if he'll have me."

The minister's face hardened. "To forbid that would be useless, I know," he said. "You will do as you choose. But I will not approve it. It will be the greatest mistake you can make."

"I love him, Papa," she said, turning away. "That can be no mistake."

XVI

Walker Rohle, from his window, saw King Overmeyer and the balance of his OX crew ride in and pull to a halt before the Trail Queen. He threw a quick glance down the street to the jail, to see if Kennicott had made an appearance and was coming to broach the big Texan as he had Dave Seringo and the others. But the marshal was not in sight. Evidently he was busy elsewhere at that moment; he knew it was not any personal doubt or fear that kept the lawman off the street. He did not believe there was anything from which Kennicott would back down. But he was glad he was not around at the moment; this would afford him a chance to talk things over with King before the clash came.

He waited until he was certain Overmeyer was inside the saloon, undoubtedly listening by then to a report of Seringo's arrest from his men. He turned to Clete McCoy, lounging comfortably in one of the deep, leather chairs.

"Get Crandall and Dry. I want them up here in fifteen minutes. No sooner, no later."

He wanted first to discuss matters with Overmeyer. Then he would need the two merchants on hand to complete what he had in mind to do. Not that he couldn't go through with it single-handed if he so desired—he simply wanted the other merchants stringing along so it would look good to the rest of the town.

McCoy grunted, got up, and crossed the room. Rohle let him out and bolted the door behind him. He had scarcely turned away when a loud, insistent hammering fell upon the paneling. That would be Overmeyer. His weighty hand was recognizable anytime. He swung the door back. Overmeyer, a huge, leather-faced man with small eyes and weather-scoured features, pushed in angrily.

"What the hell's this about Dave bein' locked up in the jug? You runnin' this town or ain't you?"

Rohle closed the door softly, closing out the grinning faces waiting expectantly on the balcony. He flushed a little at the implication and moved to his private bar.

"How about a drink of good whiskey?"

Overmeyer glared at him. He waited until the tumbler was poured, brim full, accepted it, and pivoted to the window.

"Seems I remember you sayin' this town was open to me and my boys," he rumbled. "Now I find one of them in jail and the rest ordered off the street. You better have some good reasons, Rohle, else I'll turn them loose and take this burg apart, board by board."

Typical of King Overmeyer, Rohle thought. Force, always brute force. It was the only thing the man understood. His voice faintly edged with sarcasm, he said: "I recall you tried to do that once before. Kennicott stopped you cold."

"Maybe so," Overmeyer said. "But I didn't have Dave Seringo on my payroll then."

Rohle shrugged. "He's not doing so good, either. He's been in jail since the minute he rode in."

The cattleman took a deep swallow of his bourbon. He shook his head. "There's some good reason for that. Nobody gets the drop on Dave."

"Kennicott did," Rohle said in that same cool way. He could not explain it to himself but he was deriving a weird sort of satisfaction from throwing Kennicott into Overmeyer's teeth, making him realize he was not so invincible as he would like all others to believe.

The Texan leveled a sharp glance upon him. "Say, what's goin' on around here? You said you'd got rid of Kennicott. Now you're braggin' around like he was your boy. What sort of a crooked game is this?"

Rohle refilled the big man's glass. "Nothing's wrong, nothing's changed. Just one of those little slip-ups that sometimes happen. I'll have it straightened out in a few more minutes." He had not realized he was putting it on so strongly.

"Well, let's get at it. I'm not lettin' Dave sweat it out there in no jail while the rest of the boys are havin' themselves a time. Either you bust him out quick or I'll take the crew and get him myself."

"He'll be out in thirty minutes," Rohle said.

Overmeyer looked the saloonman over speculatively. He was still in his trail clothes—Levi's, coarse shirt, dusty boots, and travel-stained hat. Rohle met his gaze. "You look like you could use a bath and a shave. Go on down to the barbershop and enjoy it while I handle this matter of Dave Seringo and the marshal. Or ex-marshal."

The Texas wagged his head. "Nope. I'll just hold off till I see that Dave's out."

Rohle frowned but nodded agreement. Overmeyer was a tough one to handle. That could mean problems in the future if they were to work together. The cattleman was more arrogant than ever now that he had Seringo working for him. What was it that had made him so cocksure he could handle the Texan? Perhaps it was the Overmeyer he remembered before Seringo entered the picture.

There was a rap on the door. Rohle crossed over and admitted Dry and Keith Crandall, both breathing heavily from fast walking. McCoy was just behind them, but the saloon owner shook his head and motioned for him to wait outside. With Overmeyer still at the window, Rohle made his introductions.

He got immediately to the point. "King's a little unhappy over one of his men being locked up in our jail. I can't say I blame him."

"Either you get him out or me and the boys will," the cattleman said.

Rohle did not remove his eyes from the Texan. To the merchants he continued: "Since Kennicott refused to resign, I consider him under suspension. He has no authority to place anyone under arrest. He can't do anything but step aside and allow anyone we appoint to take over."

"Jeff Wallis," Crandall suggested.

"Good as anybody," Rohle said. "Now, I propose that we, representing the councilmen, call upon Mark Kennicott and advise him of our decision. Are we together on this?"

"We are," Jim Dry said.

Crandall nodded.

"Then, let's do it now," Rohle said, putting his half empty glass on the bar.

Overmeyer, silent since the delivery of his ultimatum, followed after Rohle, setting his own tumbler beside that of the saloonman's.

"Make yourself at home, King," Rohle said, reaching for his hat. "Pour yourself another drink. This won't take but a few minutes."

Overmeyer grinned. "Reckon I and a few of the boys will just mosey along with you," he drawled. "Just in case all them fancy words don't work and you need a little help. Could be," he added as an afterthought, "I know this Kennicott better'n you do."

Rohle considered the cattleman's words in silence while Crandall and Dry waited. He shrugged. "Possibly," he said finally. "However, there's one thing you should understand. We are doing this in an orderly fashion. Entirely according to law. We want no trouble."

"Impressin' the citizens, eh?" Overmeyer laughed. "You're a smart one, Walker. I get the idea. But we'll just tag along anyway to see the show. Don't you be forgettin' one of my boys is the reason for all this ruckus."

Rohle moved his shoulders again. He could see it was useless to argue the point. King Overmeyer would have his way no matter what. He pulled on his hat and opened the door, wondering in that moment how much cash it would require to buy Dave Seringo's allegiance away from the Texan. It was a marvelous thing the way a man like Seringo built up another's confidence. It gave him the strength and courage to dare anything or anyone. He could use Dave Seringo. With the little gunman backing his play he could do anything he wanted to. He decided again he would have that private talk with Dave.

XVII

Jeff Wallis was standing in the doorway of the jail when the delegation walked up. Kennicott was off somewhere in the town, still looking for Curly Dan Sprewl, not fully convinced the baby-faced gunman had departed. Reaching inside, he picked up one of the shotguns, laid it across his breast in his folded arms, and barred the way of anyone who would try to enter.

"Where's Kennicott?" Rohle said, moving closer. Keith Crandall fell into step behind him.

"Hold it right there!" Wallis said. "Maybe he's inside."

"Reckon he ain't," one of the OX riders piped up. "Ain't that him comin' down the street?"

All heads swung to that point. Kennicott was fifty yards away, walking ramrod-straight and angry. Keith Crandall slid in beside Wallis.

"You want that job, now's your chance. It's all been decided. You just keep out of what happens here now. Don't make no moves to help Kennicott. We ain't asking you to hurt him . . . just stay out of it."

Wallis half lifted the shotgun as if to strike the merchant with it. Crandall's continuing words checked him.

"Kennicott's through, no matter what. No use queering your own chance by doing the wrong thing now."

He stepped away as the marshal, pushing boldly through the half circle of OX riders, elbowed his route to the doorway and faced the crowd.

Overmeyer said: "Howdy, Marshal. Right nice seein' you again."

Kennicott ignored the greeting. He let his glance travel over the group: Rohle, Crandall, Jim Dry. They were the leaders, along with Overmeyer, of course. Lockridge, Leo Kane, Humboldt the banker were missing and he gave this a moment's thought, wondering if they had changed their opinions. It wasn't likely, he concluded. Rohle just didn't figure their presence was necessary. His eyes settled on the saloonman.

"Well?"

"Kennicott," Rohle began, "since you saw fit to ignore the wishes of the town council and resign, I am hereby serving notice on you that you are suspended from your job as town marshal. As of this minute you no longer are working for the town."

"I heard earlier I was suspended. Why all the fancy words now?"

"You hadn't been officially notified," Rohle said. "We did come to an agreement this morning."

A bitter smile crossed Kennicott's lean face. "Try again, Rohle," he said softly. "Now, break this up. Get off the street unless you want some trouble."

"You'll run us in, that it, Marshal?" Overmeyer asked with a wicked grin. "Take a fair-size jail to hold all of us."

"I'll manage," Kennicott said. "Anyway, there's plenty of open ground to run you across. I can sure do that, just like I did once before."

Rohle shook his head. "You'll do no such thing, Kennicott. Since you're no longer town marshal, you have no authority to do anything like that. Fact is, the gun you're carrying makes you a law-breaker."

"Reckon your tail's sure been salted, mister," Overmeyer said.

Kennicott's gaze was on Rohle. Through tight lips he said: "Get this straight. I'm not resigning. I'm standing pat."

"That's what you think," Rohle said. "We can do it and we have done it."

"And if you don't think so just take a look to your left there," Jim Dry added with obvious satisfaction.

Kennicott shifted his eyes to the left. He had thought Jeff Wallis was standing there. But it was Clete McCoy, his mouth pulled down to a hard line, his gun drawn and leveled at Kennicott's middle. Somehow Wallis had been taken out of the play. He turned to his right. It was the same there. One of Overmeyer's riders was covering him from that angle. He was caught between the two.

121

"Go ahead, Marshal," McCoy said. "Make a move. I'd like to square up for yesterday."

Rohle waved a hand at him, silencing him. "You see, Kennicott," he said then to the lawman, "we tried to handle this in a civilized way, but you wouldn't have it so. Naturally we have to do the next best thing. Where's Wallis?"

The deputy came through the doorway of the jail, keeping his eyes straight ahead. He paused slightly ahead of Kennicott.

"Jeff, the council decided to appoint you as marshal to fill the vacancy. When the mayor returns, he will make it permanent. Take that star off Kennicott and pin it on."

There was a long, dragging moment of indecision on the part of the deputy. Then he swung slowly to meet Mark Kennicott's eyes. Apparently he saw no answer there, nor any help.

Crandall, impatient, said: "Come on, Jeff. The job's yours. The badge goes with it. Kennicott won't be needing it any more."

Wallis tarried no longer. Resting the shotgun against the door frame, he reached up, unpinned the star, and transferred it to his own breast.

"Your first official job will be to disarm the ex-marshal," Rohle said.

Clete McCoy did not wait for Wallis to comply. He stepped quickly forward and lifted Kennicott's heavy .45 from its holster and tossed it onto the desk inside the jail.

"Now, Mister Marshal," Overmeyer said, "I expect your next job better be turnin' Dave Seringo loose. I'd hate to tear up your jail before you get a chance to use it."

Wallis hesitated uncertainly. Again he lifted his glance to Kennicott.

"Keep him in there," the lawman advised. "You've got yourself some real trouble once he's out. And you'd better collect the rest of those guns."

"Turn Seringo free," Rohle ordered summarily. "You have no legal charge against him."

Wallis waited out another long minute and then, avoiding Kennicott's gaze, swung into the jail. There was a clatter of metal against metal and a short time later Dave Seringo came through the doorway, thrusting his gun into its holster as he did so. A chorus of greetings went up from the crowd. Seringo nodded but there was no friendliness in the gunman's eyes.

He came to a stop beside Kennicott, raking the tall lawman slowly with his glance. "I've got something to square with you, friend," he said in a voice that carried throughout the crowd.

Kennicott shrugged. "Any time you say. Might as well be now. You've got plenty of friends around."

Seringo's face stiffened and his eyes closed down as anger rushed through him. But he caught himself. "I'll pick the time," he promised softly. "And the place." He swung about to Jeff Wallis, standing in the doorway. "It appears you're the new marshal. How about making me your deputy?"

A yell lifted from the OX riders at the suggestion. King Overmeyer said: "Mighty good idea. Appoint Dave the deputy marshal and he'll see that things is done right around this town, eh, Walker?"

Rohle frowned at the thought. But there was no denying the Texan and his crew, who were looking on the matter as a huge joke. He nodded to Wallis who took the deputy badge from his pocket and handed it to Seringo. To Rohle he said: "How about the swearing in?"

"God dammit, Dave Seringo, you're the deputy marshal!" King Overmeyer roared. "That's all the swearin' in he needs. Come on, you saddle warmers, we'll make Dave buy a round of drinks to celebrate his appointment. This sure is the first time a OX man was on that side of the law."

"One thing I've got to do first," Seringo said, sliding a glance

123

over the group. "I reckon you could call it my first official job."

He wheeled suddenly on Kennicott. His gun came up swiftly, smoothly, a flashing arc in the sunlight. It struck Kennicott hard alongside the head, just behind the ear. The lawman's knees buckled and he dropped soundlessly.

"One I owed you," Seringo said coolly, and replaced his weapon. He lifted his colorless eyes to Wallis. "Lock him up good, Marshal. He's my own private prisoner and I'll be wantin' to see him later. I've got a little unfinished business that'll need takin' care of about the time we ride out."

"Lock him up for what?" Jeff Wallis demanded. "What's he done?"

"Lock him up because I said so," Seringo replied. "You need a better reason?"

Wallis glanced beyond Seringo to Walker Rohle. The saloonman shrugged and nodded slightly. Jim Dry was looking off down the street. Crandall was studying the backs of his hands. Neither man, plainly, wanted anything to do with any decision. With a faint sigh Wallis moved to help Kennicott back to his feet. He paused as Seringo laid a hand upon his shoulder.

"Lock him up tight, old man. If I find him gone when I come lookin' for him, you're a dead badge-toter."

The crowd turned away and started for the Trail Queen. One man halted suddenly and faced Seringo.

"Deputy Marshal," he said with overdrawn seriousness, "is it all right with you if we go back and get our artillery? We sure do feel naked without it."

Seringo stroked his pointed chin thoughtfully, making a show of it. "Well, now it sure ain't fittin' you boys should run around naked. I reckon, if you figure to behave, it will be all right. But you got to remember one thing. It's sure not right to shoot at each other. It ain't brotherly. Now, if it's somebody else, the law'll overlook it. But don't you go poppin' away at each other."

"Yes, sir, Mister Deputy Marshal," the cowboy said. "We hereby gives you our solemn promise."

With a laugh he swung back toward the jail, followed by the other OX men who had been disarmed earlier by Kennicott and Jeff Wallis. They were still laughing about it when they turned into the building.

XVIII

Walker Rohle paused and watched the jag of OX men cut back toward the jail. There was a light frown pulling at his brows, showing not only his displeasure at the turn of events but also a vague worry. King Overmeyer and his crew were far worse than he had bargained for; they were every bit as bad as Kennicott had said. He had thought, originally, to control the men through Overmeyer, but that was proving an absurdity for the Texan was no better than the worst of his crew.

It was a price he must now pay. There was no backing down if his play was to be successful. And it would be worth it, he assured himself. Often it required drastic measures to bring about a desired end just as a surgeon sometimes was compelled to knife deeply in order to save a life. This was one such instance. It was all justified and in the end matters would work out right. He kept his eyes on the doorway of the jail as those thoughts moved through his mind. He watched, almost with caught breath, for any signs of trouble, listening for sounds of violence. He was not too sure of Jeff Wallis and he knew Overmeyer's men were itching for an excuse to start something.

At his shoulder he heard Keith Crandall say: "Thanks for the drink, Mister Overmeyer, but I think I'll pass it up. Got a mite of work I ought to get done before dark."

"Hell with that!" Overmeyer bellowed. "You got to have one drink with the new deputy town marshal! That's a order from him! You want to buck your deputy's orders, friend?"

"No . . . I reckon not," Crandall replied in a falling voice. Rohle smiled thinly. Crandall was disturbed, too. The work he referred to probably meant he wanted to get things under cover before any of the OX cowboys paid his store a whirlwind visit of destruction. Likely he planned to close up and lock the doors. Not that it would do any good. Nothing would stop the trail hands once they took a notion to try something. He had his wonder about Crandall then, wonder if he was losing his courage and would be trying to back down now that the final hour had arrived.

Probably he would. Men like Crandall talked big, but when things got tight, all their sand ran out. A faint sneer on his lips, he turned to Dry. "How about you, Jim? Lost your thirst, too?"

"Not me," the merchant said quickly. "I sure could use a snort. Come on, let's get it."

Overmeyer and his crew had not slowed but moved on. They had reached the Trail Queen and were wheeling onto the porch when Rohle's attention came back to them.

"The back way, Jim," he murmured to Dry.

The merchant swung a startled look at him. "What about Overmeyer? Might stir him up for sure, if he sees us taking off by ourselves."

Rohle said: "Overmeyer's not scaring me much. And I choose my own drinking partners."

It was near the middle of the afternoon. Dry had gone his cautious way down the back stairs and Rohle was sitting at his desk, debating the merits of walking over to the parsonage for a call on Judith when a yell went up from the street below. He got quickly to his feet and hurried to the window. Two of Overmeyer's cowpunchers were standing in front of Dry's store, whirling their lasso ropes overhead, the target being the saddle and harness display horse of the merchant's.

"Watch me git that old dapple hoss!" one of the riders was shouting. "Always wanted me a purty one like him!"

"Don't you fling no loop over my hoss!" the other warned. "He's sure mine and I'm aimin' to have him!"

Both ropes settled over the pressed paper and wood model, landing accurately about the neck. Another yell went up and both men began to pull. The display came over with a crash, the head breaking free and rolling awkwardly into the dust.

Dry immediately came plunging through the doorway to protest. He halted abruptly when he saw the grinning men and the half a dozen more who had gathered behind them.

"Now, see here," he said, "you quit that. You can't destroy my property. I'll have the law on you."

One of the cowpunchers, calmly recoiling his rope, laughed. "Sure, old man, you go tell the law about it. You'll find him over there in the saloon with King and the rest of the waddies. Meantime, I'll just do a little mite of practicin' hog-tyin' you. That old stuffed gray hoss of your'n is sort of peaked."

Giving his rope two fast twirls, he sent it reaching for the merchant. Dry side-stepped hastily, his face red.

"Ain't you goin' to tell the law about this, pop?" one of the men asked.

Dry lifted his hands in a gesture of helplessness. "I don't figure it would do much good," he said, and went back into his store.

"Now, he's sure right," the man with the rope said. "This here is our town for dang' certain."

The group began to split up, to drift apart, drawn by different and new attractions. Some headed for other saloons, some for the sporting houses that stood at the west end of town. Shouts and laughter ran along the street, and now and then a surprised yell or one of pain. Somewhere glass shattered, either an accident or a deliberate act.

Down near the stable the rapid beat of hoofs drew Rohle's attention. Two riders, evidently engaged in an impromptu horse race, came up the street at a thundering run. They were yelling at the tops of their voices and flogging their mounts mercilessly as they passed, adding to that with sporadic firings of their pistols. A rolling cloud of yellow dust followed them as they sped by. Two men, hidden from view by the porch roof just below, staggered out in the wake of the racers, carrying the sign Alf Wisdom and Cable had tacked to the front of the building. They had it stretched between them, upside down, and now, rallying a round of onlookers, they began a noisy parade.

At the precise moment they reached the corner where Jergenson's Café stood, Curly Osgood, a cowpuncher from one of the nearby spreads, came out. He walked across the street for Kane's livery stable, cutting directly in front of the shouting paraders. Immediately one of the OX men rushed forward to turn him back. When he seized Osgood's arm, the burly young cowboy tagged him sharply with a wide swinging right fist and knocked him to the ground.

He was up at once with his friends gathering quickly around in a tight circle, yelling advice and much encouragement. But the OX rider was no match for Osgood, who drove him to earth as regularly as he arose. When the man was no longer able to get to his feet, Osgood swung back to his errand. Three other OX cowboys immediately rushed him.

They struck him in a single solid-fronted formation, carrying him down into the dust. Leo Kane came then from the depths of the stable with a shotgun. The fighting ceased at once. Osgood got slowly to his feet, brushing at his clothing with his wide-brimmed hat. The OX men glared at Kane and Rohle speculated momentarily on the possibility of real trouble, but Overmeyer's men lost interest quickly and turned away, coming toward the Trail Queen. The canvas sign remained where it had been dropped, now a dirty, trampled invitation ground into the dust.

Another brawl was apparently in progress down below. Rohle could hear the crash of furniture, the faint tinkle of shattering glass. Kennicott had certainly been right; Overmeyer and his crowd were more than just rough and wild. They were wreckers, destroyers. If things kept on at this rate, he would be forced to talk to Overmeyer about it, remind him of their agreement.

The sounds of the struggle beneath ceased. He returned his attention to the window. The two who had participated in the horse race were returning, their mounts lathered and blowing foam from their nostrils. Suddenly the men halted, something farther along seizing their attention.

"Look out!" one yelled, and both swerved for the sidewalk.

It was another race, this time between two wagons, or, rather, a wagon and a buggy. Rohle stared at the latter vehicle. It was Doc Cartwright's but it certainly was not the little medical man doing the driving. An OX man held the reins. The other, a light buckboard, had its owner still aboard, clinging tightly to the back of the seat while an OX cowboy stood, like a chariot driver, and plied the whip to the frantic horses.

They swept by the saloon in a shrill burst of cheering and a rattle of gunfire. The buckboard suddenly yawed widely and spilled over. Cartwright's dusty, black rig flew on and was soon blocked from Rohle's view.

The owner of the buckboard got dazedly to his feet and staggered toward his vehicle. The OX cowpunchers had stopped its spinning wheels and together had placed their shoulders against it, righting it once more. The man was helped to his seat with elaborate care and attention, the reins thrust into his numbed fingers. Then, with a shout and a blast of gunfire, the fellow was sent on his way. The last Rohle saw of the unwilling contestant was the rear of the buckboard swinging crazily down the street while the driver fought to slow the runaway team.

He remained at the window, watching a group of trail hands methodically overturning and kicking in the benches some of the merchants had placed along the street for the use of women customers and finally, sick of the scene, closed the window and turned away. He crossed to his bar and poured himself a generous portion of bourbon.

He glanced to the hands of the thick watch carried in his vest pocket. Afternoon. Only afternoon—and the night was yet to come. The worst was yet ahead.

XIX

Sitting on the hard cell cot in the jail, Mark Kennicott stared thoughtfully at Jeff Wallis. The deputy, turned away from him, was sunk deep into the chair before the desk, his eyes lost on the patch of sky visible through the window. The blow Seringo had dealt him had been a glancing one, stunning him only momentarily, and his present awareness of it was no more than a slight throbbing behind his ear and a slightly raised place.

What troubled him most was Jeff Wallis. He was finding it difficult, nearly impossible, to understand the man. Twice he had tried to talk to the deputy about the events of the afternoon and twice he had been coldly ignored. Now, a deep suspicion was brooding within his mind, a disturbing thought that Wallis had deliberately and intentionally left his side during the meeting with Rohle and Overmeyer's crowd, thus greasing the way for Clete McCoy to slide in and throw a gun on him.

But why? Had Wallis suddenly gone over to Walker Rohle's side? Had a terrible fear for his own safety caused him to switch allegiance?

Kennicott shook his head wearily. Outside in the street there was a burst of shooting and then yelling. Two riders thundered by in a reckless race and some time after that Doc Cartwright's buggy careened past the open doorway. Kennicott had never known the doctor to drive his rig in such fashion before and he had his suspicions as to who was actually holding the reins. King Overmeyer's trail hands were having their way with the town, that was certain.

And that Jeff Wallis had no intention of interfering with them also was plain. What could the man be thinking of? He was the legal law in the town, a deputy if not actually the marshal—why didn't he do something about it? Give those OX hands another three or four hours of hard drinking and unopposed hell-raising and by midnight Cameo Crossing would become a shambles, something from which it would never recover.

He decided to appeal to Wallis once more. "Jeff," he called, rising and moving to the bar grating, "you've got to do something about that out there. You just can't sit here and let that bunch run wild. It will soon be dark, and, if you don't get them slowed down a bit by then, you won't be able to do anything with them."

The deputy seemed not to hear. He remained silent, lost in the contemplation of the horizon beyond the town. "I know you're not afraid of them but if you want somebody to side you, let me out of here, and I'll give you a hand."

The thought that Kennicott might believe him a coward brought Wallis to life. He swung about in his chair, his face pale, his eyes angry.

"I ain't a-feared of them saddle bums, and you know it. But I ain't planning on suicide, either. Not for this town. Maybe you don't see it, but it looks to me like this is just what Walker Rohle wants. Somebody to bust up the place so's he can walk in and pick up the pieces all for himself when it's done with."

Kennicott shook his head. "That makes no sense, Jeff. And Rohle's not the only one in this town. There's a lot of other people, men, women, and kids. They don't think like Rohle does."

Ray Hogan

"Then where the hell are they?" Wallis said. "Why ain't they here? Where was they when that bunch come marching down the street a while ago? I'll danged quick tell you where they are . . . all down in their holes, too danged scared to say anything. The town don't mean a thing to them."

"It's not their business to stand up and face the Dave Seringos and men like those who work for OX. You know that, Jeff. That's what we were hired to do."

Wallis shrugged. "You heard my orders. Lock you up and stay put. That's just what I'm doing. What happens out there in the street ain't no affair of mine."

"Orders you know are wrong," Kennicott said in a patient voice. "You're the law here now. It's up to you to enforce it. Either do it or let me out of here so I can. It will be pure hell around here after dark if somebody doesn't do something."

"This is the way they wanted it and this is sure the way they'll get it. Maybe I've learned something in my life, Mark, that you haven't. You can't fight men like Rohle, the big men who run things. They hold all the cards and you can't win. Best thing for people like you and me is to just stand by and wait. Give them enough rope and they'll. . . ."

"But a lot of people will get hurt waiting for that day," Kennicott broke in wearily. "I can't figure you out, Jeff. Somehow I figured you wrong."

There was a heavy footstep at the door and he paused, looking up. It was George Lockridge. The tall minister hesitated for a moment, and then entered, moving to where he could face Wallis. There was a sharp glint in his eyes and his mouth worked with a bridled fury.

"What's the meaning of this, Marshal? Why aren't you out there doing your duty? This vandalism must be stopped, and, if you don't make them put away their guns, someone is going to get killed or hurt."

132

Wallis swept the dark-clad figure with a withering glance. "Seems to me you was the one who kept saying there wasn't no harm in such goings-on. That trail hands wasn't bad at all like we made out they were."

"I said they didn't need to be murdered. They're just boys . . . young men having fun. They must be curbed, that's all."

"Well, now, maybe a little of that sweetness and light business of yours just might do the trick," Wallis said sarcastically. "Suppose you trot out there and try a little out on them."

Lockridge shook his head. "You know I could get nowhere with them. And it is beside the point. It is your job and responsibility. You were appointed town marshal and it's up to you."

"Not me," Wallis said. "My orders was to stay here and guard my prisoner. That's just what I'm figuring to do."

"Whose orders?"

"Your leading citizen, Mister Walker Rohle. And a couple of others he's cottoned up to."

Lockridge shifted his gaze toward the cell, to Mark Kennicott. A frown knitted his brow. "I'm not sure I understand. It doesn't make any sense."

"Then maybe you better go have a little confab with Rohle," Wallis suggested. "You wanted it this way. You and the others. You got any complaints about the way it's turning out, I figure you ought to handle them yourselves."

Kennicott said: "You stay off the street, Lockridge. Don't try to see Rohle. No time for you to be walking about."

The minister eyed Kennicott. "Why are you locked up?"

"So Dave Seringo can drop by when he has a spare moment and put a bullet in him, that's why," Wallis answered quickly.

"Kill him?"

"What else? Just a cute trick one of your playful cowboys wants to pull. Them same cowboys that never hurt nobody."

Lockridge was visibly shaken. He returned his gaze to the deputy. "I just don't understand it. Something's terribly wrong here. This isn't what we had in mind. Of that I'm sure."

"Maybe it isn't what you were thinking," Wallis said, "but it's sure what Rohle and his crowd were figuring on."

"Just what do you mean by that?"

"That you've been took, Reverend. You've been handed a real short count. They was using you for a blind to get what they wanted. Maybe you thought you knew what you was talking about, only you didn't. You were wrong a mile."

Lockridge stiffened. His tanned face lost its color. He wheeled about and marched through the doorway into the street. Somewhere, down near Kane's, a man screamed in pain, and then there were two quick gunshots.

"You see the way of it, Jeff," Kennicott said softly. "Rohle took them all in. We can't let him get away with it."

"Ain't much I can do now."

"There's plenty you can do. Let me out of here and give me a gun, for one thing. Then I've got a show if Seringo comes back. And I'll give you a hand out there on the street."

"I was thinking about Seringo . . . what I said to the parson there a minute ago. Doing what he said I had to do would be nothing but murder."

Wallis, partly turned away from Kennicott, glanced down at the star pinned to his vest. He brushed at it with the cuff of his coarse shirt. Watching him, Kennicott had his first glimmer of understanding.

"That the reason for all this, Jeff? Your wanting to be marshal? That what made you step away this afternoon and let McCoy come in on my side?"

"They told me you was through anyway, no matter what you did," Wallis answered. "Said if I'd just keep my hand out, nobody'd get hurt and the job would be mine. Made sense when they was telling it to me."

A rush of anger flashed through Kennicott. His own deputy turned against him. Wasn't there anyone a man could trust—could depend on? Seething words of denunciation crowded to his lips but after a moment he checked them, choked them back. Any man could get off on the wrong trail and make a mistake, any man whose dreams outreached his judgment.

"Looks like they took you in, too, Jeff," he said. "Just like they have Lockridge and the others."

"Could be," the deputy admitted.

"Then how about letting me out of here?"

Jeff Wallis shook his head. "Just don't see how I can, Mark. You're my friend and all that, but they made me the law and my orders was to keep you locked up. But don't you worry none about Seringo. I'll see he don't get no chance to cut you down without you having some say-so."

"I'm not worrying about myself," Kennicott said. "I'm thinking about this town. And the people in it."

"I reckon they asked for it," Jeff Wallis said, and turned away.

XX

Another brawl was in progress on the street. Two OX riders wrestled ineffectually back and forth as each tried to throw the other to the ground. Rohle watched them without interest. This was the sort of harmless horseplay he had told the others they could expect from trail hands—not the deliberate and mean vandalism and dangerous shooting they were witnessing.

Overmeyer was not standing up to his agreement. He was failing completely to keep his men in hand or else he willfully was allowing them to have their way, ignoring the understanding he and Rohle had. The crash of a splintering chair below brought him up sharply. He swung about immediately and, leaving the room, went downstairs to the bar.

Overmeyer, his elbows hooked on the rim of the mahogany counter, had just completed one of his stories. The dozen or so men grouped around him in a half circle were laughing uproariously. Rohle paused at the bottom of the steps and glanced over the room. About a third of the Texan's crew was in the building, standing at the bar or playing cards at the tables. There was none of the Trail Queen's regular patrons in evidence. One stranger, a baby-faced, curly-headed kid, sat at a corner table, nursing a bottle and talking with one of the girls.

"Hey, there, Walker, old stud!" Overmeyer greeted him, with a wave of his hand. The cattleman was flushed, smiling broadly, and he rolled somewhat from the load of liquor he was carrying. "How about a drink with the best damn' trail crew in Texas?"

Rohle left the stairs and moved up in front of Overmeyer. He glanced at the circle of faces that closed in about him. Hard, belligerent faces, all looking for any reason to start trouble.

"I thought maybe you and I might have a drink up in my rooms. Talk things over a bit," he said, managing a smile.

"What's wrong with right here?" Overmeyer said. "What's good enough for my boys is good enough for me. I've always said that, ain't I, boys?"

There was a deafening affirmative chorus.

"Now, whatever you got to say, why, you just spit it out right here and now. I sure ain't got nothin' to hide from my boys."

Again Rohle glanced about the saloon. His eyes caught the pile of broken chairs and tables pushed into one corner by the swamper, the door to a back room ripped loose and sagging from one twisted hinge, the bucket of broken glassware standing near the rear exit. The sight of those things made him angry and brave.

"I want to talk to you about your men," he said in a loud voice. "When I agreed to open up the town to you, it was on the understanding that you and your crew would have some respect for property. There was to be no shooting, no harm to any of the citizens. Everybody was to have a good time and enjoy themselves. But those men of yours are running wild out there in the street. They're fighting and shooting and breaking up everything they can lay their hands on."

"Do tell," Overmeyer said.

"You've got to stop them. Not only are they causing hundreds of dollars damage in the street but they're doing it right here in my place."

"You mean my boys have been wreckin' your saloon?" Overmeyer asked in wonderment. "Doin' things like this?" he added, and, taking a half empty quart bottle of whiskey, hurled it over his shoulder. It struck nearly dead center of a large section of backbar mirror, bringing it down in a shimmering crash.

Rohle was surprised. A shout went up from the OX men in the room. Another bottle came twisting through the air and struck the framework, missing the adjoining mirror but dislodging a shelf of glasses.

Overmeyer unsteadily lifted his hands. "Now, listen here, boys. Mister Rohle don't want us doin' nothin' like that. I was just bein' sure that was what he meant."

Rohle, his face white, said: "I'll expect pay for that, King. And anything else that's broken in here."

"Expectin' ain't gettin'," the cattleman said. "And don't go gettin' hard-nosed about things, else we'll give you something to really bawl about. Right now we're just havin' us a time, funnin' like. But you get us mad and we'll tree this town like you never saw a town treed."

"You agreed. . . ."

"Agreed, hell! We've been waitin' for the chance to come back to this stinkin' place and make up for last time when that marshal of yours wouldn't let us hold over. We're goin' to have us just twice as much celebratin' and by the time we leave here tomorrow this town is goin' to be ours, hoof, horns, and tail. We'll have it roped and branded with an OX iron . . . and that includes the women, too."

Rohle stared at the Texan's bloated face. The words he was hearing were product of a dream, vague, indistinct. Kennicott had been right! These men were savages, brutes without conscience. And he was powerless to do anything about it. Only Kennicott had the ability and strength to cope with their kind— and Mark Kennicott was locked in a cell.

The impulse to hurry out and down the street and free the marshal, begging him to take over, swept through him. To make an offer to help him, to recruit men to back him up in what had to be done. Subconsciously he immediately rejected that idea. Could he ever do that? It would be an admission of defeat, of failure, and his incapacity to control his own progeny. Wordlessly he turned toward the stairway.

Overmeyer's mocking voice trailed after him. "You best keep to your room, Walker boy. Sure wouldn't want you to get them there fine clothes all mussed up."

Rohle struggled to maintain his dignity. He was discovering, in those moments, what it was like to hold a tiger by the tail.

XXI

At about the same moment King Overmeyer was hurling the heavy whiskey bottle into the mirror at the Trail Queen, George Lockridge entered the parsonage. He hung his narrow-brimmed black hat on the four-pronged hall tree in the small foyer and strode into the parlor, his long face solemn and knotted in deep thought and worry.

His first impulse, upon leaving the jail, was to call upon Rohle and demand an explanation for the turn of events in Cameo Crossing, but he had reconsidered. For one thing he felt he needed to think further about matters before he boldly broached the saloonkeeper and, too, he was remembering Kennicott's clipped words: *Stay off the street. Don't try to see Rohle. No time for you to be walking about.* And somewhere in his mind there was a growing, persistent suspicion that the lawman had been right, that he knew whereof he spoke. But still he was reluctant to accept the unwelcome admission. In actuality, it was a lifelong weakness of his, being forever unable to face up to a problem when he had erred; it cast him adrift in a sea of conflictions wherein he floundered helplessly.

Now, here in Cameo Crossing, things had not turned out the way he had expected at all. He had thought the removal of Mark Kennicott from office would be the answer to all mortal problems that faced the town. Somehow it had not. What had happened? He dropped wearily into a chair and laid his arms across his knees, considering his clasped hands. He was still in that position when, a few minutes later, he heard a sound behind him and, turning, saw Judith there with a question in her eyes.

"What is it, Papa?"

He shook his head in a hopeless sort of way. "I just don't know, I just don't know," he said.

"Have you discovered we have no marshal at all now?" she asked. Earlier Jim Dry had brought them the news of the change.

Lockridge looked up at her, deep pain in his eyes. He had not missed the implication lying behind her question. "We have a marshal, all right," he said. "Jeff Wallis. But he refuses to do anything about those men in the street. He said he had orders to leave them alone."

"And Mark?"

"Locked up in jail."

"Locked up," she said. "Why?"

"I received no answer that made sense to me. Something about his being kept there so a man named Seringo could come later and kill him."

Judith came farther into the room and sank into a chair. Her face had gone dead white and her eyes mirrored the fear clutching her heart. "I . . . I don't understand," she said.

George Lockridge got to his feet. "Nor do I," he said. "Wallis said this was all Walker Rohle's planning. That he actually intended for things to be this way."

Judith was silent. She was recalling many things Mark Kennicott had said. She had paid them scant attention at the time, but now she was realizing how close to gospel truth they had been. He had been predicting the future accurately and he had known far more about the way of men than she or her father had given him credit for. And she remembered something else— what Kennicott had said about her father being the cause of many innocent people being hurt due to his ideas.

She turned to watch her father, slowly coming to the realization that he, too, was reaching. He had been duped by Walker Rohle and the others. They had used him to cloak, in respectability, their own plans. He was finding it hard to admit, even to himself. She could see the beads of sweat standing out on his wide forehead as he nervously rubbed a clenched fist into an open palm.

But what was done was done? Mark was in jail, awaiting vengeance by a gunman he had sought to protect the town from. Someone must act, do something. And quickly.

"Papa," she said then, "there's only one thing to do. Get Mark out of jail. He's the only one who can do anything about this . . . if he will after the way he has been treated. There's no one else we can trust."

Lockridge seemed not to hear. "I can't see what is wrong," he muttered in that desperate, lost tone. "This is not the way it was planned to be. And why won't Walker let the new marshal act? That's what I cannot understand."

Judith settled her gaze upon him. She could see the old

indecision of days long ago clouding his eyes once more, something she had thought and hoped they had left far behind them when they moved westward. But it was there, strong as ever, leaving him at loose ends.

He had always been a man to choose the wrong side, stand behind the unworthy man, shoulder the wrong cause. He was even one to join forces with someone, firmly believing all things he was told while turning a deaf ear to the other half of the question. Invariably he picked wrong and found himself eventually in a compromising position from which there was no graceful escape. Then was when he was at his worst, his lowest, in those black, critical moments when his world broke apart and tumbled down about his shoulders and left him cold and alone and with no friends at either hand.

He needed much help and consolation at such times in his life. Once there had been a wife to put her arms around him, much as you would a small child, and tell him all would be well in the end. Now it was Judith's task and on the several previous occasions she had stepped in and with brimming heart done her chore well. But this time it was different.

She was finding it difficult to muster the sympathy and compassion she knew she should exhibit. Why hadn't he looked more carefully into matters before he thundered out his denunciations? Why hadn't he listened to someone else besides Walker Rohle and those known to be allied with him? Mark Kennicott, for instance. As Mark had prophesied, he could and was now getting innocent people hurt. He could even be the indirect cause of Kennicott's death because of his bad judgment.

"We just can't sit here and mope about this!" she cried, all at once impatient. "We must do something."

"What can we do?" Lockridge moaned. "I'm useless against men like those cowboys. If I went out there on the street, they would make a fool of me."

It would be better than having someone's blood on your hands, Judith thought and was immediately shocked at her own disrespect. But something had altered within her in that last, brief portion of an hour. Or perhaps it had only come to a head, to a point of recognition. Possibly it had been building itself for years and she was now seeing for the first time what her mother had been aware of all the time—that George Lockridge was a good man but weak and ineffectual and utterly without judgment.

His ideas were those implanted by anyone who could garner his attention, his thoughts those of whomever stood in the background fostering a cause, good or bad. His actions were the mechanical shadows of anyone who pulled a string. He was any man's tool.

But the damage was done and recriminations were of little help now. She faced him. "Papa, I'm going to do something about this. I'm not standing here and letting Rohle get away with it. I've got to help Mark, somehow."

Immediately she repented the harshness of her tone. Lockridge cringed. He was so like a small child. His fear of scolding showed through his eyes. But there could be no help from him. Anything that would be done would be done by herself alone; she must think for herself. And the most important thing of all was Mark. Once free, and safe, he would handle the desperate situation the town now was in.

She paused in her frantic run of thought, reviewing the last. It sounded like words from Tom Girard's lips. She, like all the others, looked, too, to Mark Kennicott for protection and salvation. And in that reflection she had her first full understanding of the man's strong sense of duty and responsibility that he felt for the town and its people. She had been wrong all the time. It was plain now and she would tell Mark so. What a fool she had been! And to think he loved her enough to be willing to turn his back on it.

"It's wrong to kill," George Lockridge mumbled aloud, apparently also thinking of Kennicott and still trying hard to justify his own actions to himself. "It is wicked to take another's life. Sinful. I was right to denounce those who practiced such violence. That was why I demanded his removal . . . before God, that was my only reason!"

Judith crossed the room to his side. "It's all right now, Papa," she said. "Don't worry about it any more. I'll find some way to help Mark. He'll know what to do."

Tom Girard again. Leave it to Mark Kennicott. He will make all things right again. He was the magic power that overcame all evil, all odds, even a town overrun by two dozen or more drunken trail hands and gunmen in league with the most powerful merchants in the entire territory. Yes, leave it squarely up to Mark Kennicott and maybe watch him die trying to get the job done. A shudder passed through Judith.

But he would die for certain if no one came to aid and free him from that cell in the jail. Hurriedly she considered the best course to follow—go see Rohle and try to persuade him to help? That would be foolish. She knew without a second thought she could expect no help from him. Talk to the other merchants, to the townspeople themselves? That was useless, also. Either they were with Rohle or else feared him so greatly they could be expected to offer no aid.

There was one answer, no more: go to Mark and somehow help him escape. Evidently Jeff Wallis could no longer be counted upon as a friend so she must avoid him. That would be difficult but she would manage it some way. She had to manage it.

To her father she said: "I'm going to see Mark, try to help him escape. You had better stay here until I'm back. I'll bring Mark with me."

He nodded woodenly. She was not even sure he had understood her words. Or actually heard.

"I'm going over to the jail, Papa," she repeated.

That seemed to arouse him. "I'm not sure you ought to be on the street. It's getting dark and those cowboys. . . ."

"I'll go by the alley. Nobody will see me. Most of them are up at the other end of the street."

He lowered his head. "All right, Judith. All right."

She glanced at him sharply, still not convinced he fully understood. He was like a person dazed by a terrible blow. But it didn't really matter. She was better off without his attempting to help her. There, alone in the parlor, he would be safe and could get in no trouble.

She crossed the room, hurried down the hallway, through the kitchen, and opened the back door, noticing as she stepped onto the porch that it was almost fully dark. That was good. She was glad for that additional advantage of coming night. Having no fear of being out alone, she felt the shadows would enable her more easily to reach the jail without being seen and effect Mark Kennicott's escape.

XXII

Judith crossed the short length of back yard to the gate that opened into the alley, carefully avoiding the pile of trash and litter that needed hauling off and burning. The rusty hinges squealed loudly in the evening murkiness as she pushed the gate open and stepped out.

Closing it behind her, she hesitated, deciding which was the better route—circle the vacant house next door and cross the street at that point or move on down the alley, past the empty structure until she was well below all settlement, and then cross over. She settled upon the latter course since it would lessen the chances of her being seen. She started at once, hurrying along the rutted, uneven path, eyes on the ground as she sought to keep from stumbling. Thus engrossed, she did not see the dark shape arise suddenly from the deep pools of blackness behind the empty house.

She felt a strong hand clamp over her mouth. A powerful arm encircled her waist and dragged her off balance, lifting her free of the ground. She began to struggle, to kick and strike out with her hands, but she was at complete and terrible disadvantage. The attacker had taken her from behind and was holding her well aloft in his muscular arms. She could not reach him with her nails but could only kick futilely at his legs with her heels.

The man's breath was hot and foul on her neck, heavy with liquor. He was murmuring some animal-like sound from low in his throat, all the time propelling her toward the sagging, open back door of the deserted house. She fought to halt the inexorable progress but her efforts were useless.

"Now girlie, now girlie"—she could barely make out what he was saying—"don't do that."

She opened her mouth, pressed tightly by his broad, grimy hand, and strained for breath. She felt the roundness of a finger between her lips, against her teeth. Revolted by the taste she nevertheless seized the opportunity presented her. She bit down hard. Her captor ripped out an oath and jerked his hand away. Judith screamed, putting all her breath into it. Scarcely had the first sound passed her lips when his hand slapped against her mouth again, crushing back the desperate cry. The arm about her waist tightened, pressing hard upon her breasts, shooting pain all through her body. Breathing became difficult.

"Now, girlie, you just behave yourself," the animal voice rumbled in her ear. "Iffen you don't, I'll sure get mean with you."

Again she parted her teeth and clamped down upon his finger, ignoring the warning. He cursed savagely and the clamp

145

about her waist slackened. He struck her alongside the face just as the cry flung from her lips. A vicious, sharp blow that set up a ringing in her head and set lights to dancing before her eyes. Her senses spun crazily and she felt all the strength draining from her body.

"That's better, girlie."

The mumbling, fetid voice seemed far away, the words thick and slow. She became faintly aware that they were in the yard of the empty house, that she was being carried, like a small child, slowly but surely toward the yawning, black rectangle that was an open doorway.

Frantic alarm rushed through her. She reacted instinctively. But she had no strength. She could only struggle pitifully against those powerful arms and hands that held her prisoner. She managed to cry out, weakly, the sound of her voice a bare etching against the night's black surface. Again she heard the loathsome voice and felt the hot, sickening breath on her face.

"All right girlie. All right, now. Couple minutes and everything's goin' to be fine."

George Lockridge was still sitting in his chair where Judith had left him when he heard her first terrified cry. He came to his feet in a single bound, suddenly galvanized into action, and tried to recall what it was she had said to him. Where had she said she was going? He had been so engrossed in his own problem he had scarcely paid any attention. What was it? She was going somewhere—to the jail, it seemed, that she would go down the alley to avoid being seen by the OX cowboys roaming the street.

He went through the door in long, running strides and halted in the center of his own back yard. He heard a faint moan to his right. Somewhere near the old vacant Harley house that had stood open and abandoned for almost a year now. Wheeling swiftly, he strained his eyes through the darkness. He saw the dim, bulky outline of a man, bent slightly, moving slowly toward the structure. He seemed to be carrying something in his arms. In the next instant, like a throttling hand clutching his throat, he realized it was Judith the figure was holding captive.

He did not pause to wonder how he knew it was his daughter. It was actually too dark really to see. But some inner knowledge and parental intuition that is granted a man when his offspring is in grave jeopardy telegraphed the conviction to him. A half-strangled yell escaped his lips. He wheeled and raced across the littered yard, vaulting the staggering old board fence. He came down hard on a pile of rubble, reeled from the solid impact, and tripped up in a confusion of tangled, waist-high weeds.

The stocky outline of the intruder hesitated, still clutching his prize. He began to back away, unintelligible curses trickling from his mouth. It was the man, Dave Seringo.

"Let her go!" Lockridge screamed. "Let my daughter go you . . . you scum of Satan!"

The dark shape continued to retreat. Lockridge, a man suddenly berserk, lunged across the cluttered yard after him. His great hands reached out, grasping, clutching for anything. His fingers tightened upon Judith's arm and he pulled with all his strength, wrenching her free. She fell between the two, and Lockridge, tripped up again, came in hard against the man.

They crashed together, the sound of their colliding bodies a dull, meaty thud. They went full length into the weeds. The intruder struggled to draw his gun. Lockridge saw it glint in the meager light and wrapped his big hand around it. For a full minute they wrestled for the weapon's possession. Rolling, kicking, thrashing back and forth. Another hoarse cry wrenched from his lips. The gun! If only he could get the gun—he could kill this Dave Seringo, remove him from God's earth!

His voice was weird and high-pitched in his own ears. He

struck out at the evil face, wildly, savagely. He felt his knuckles smash into flesh and bone, heard the grunt of pain. The fingers on the pistol slackened and it came loosely into his own hand. He rolled quickly away, oblivious to the sharp nettles and burrs that pricked and dug into his face and neck. He sprang to his feet, dragging his lungs for breath. Holding the gun with both hands, he aimed at the now prostrate Seringo.

"I'll kill you! You hellion . . . you despoiler of women! I'll kill you!"

Hands clamped upon his own, pressing the gun aside. Judith's voice cried into his ear.

"Don't, Papa! Don't shoot him . . . don't kill him!"

The gunman was scrambling to his feet, a dim shape in the gloom. *Don't shoot! Don't kill him!* The words began to penetrate Lockridge's seething mind.

"I'm all right, Papa! I'm all right! You hear me? You understand? He's gone now. Run away. Everything's all right."

Slowly Lockridge began to calm; his turmoil-racked brain became more rational, the soaring anger dwindled. "Judith? You're all right?"

"Yes, Papa. He didn't harm me." She moved closer to him, her face a pale oval in the faint light. Her clothing was in shreds where Seringo's clawing fingers had ripped it off, her hair a tangled, disarranged mass. She smiled up at her father.

"Everything is all right now, Papa," she said again.

"I was afraid he . . . ," the minister began, and halted uncertainly. His eyes dropped to the pistol gripped so tightly in his broad hand. Slowly, incredulously he lifted his glance to Judith. "I almost killed a man. I would have, had you not stopped me."

He was cold sober now, breathing normally. He stared at his daughter. Quickly, as if he needed to say it and have done with it before his determination weakened, he said: "I've been wrong about many things, Judith. I see that now. Most of all I've been wrong about Mark Kennicott."

"You know now there are times when violence is necessary. That there are things that must be done."

He nodded slowly. "This country is a long way from Baltimore and the kind of law and order we have there. I know now there is a great difference and I realize, too, we are not ready for that sort of law yet."

"But it will come, Papa," Judith said. "If we stand behind Mark Kennicott and the men like him, it will come."

"I was a fool not to see it," Lockridge said, taking her gently by the arm. "Now, you must get back inside our house. Lock the doors and stay there."

They started down the dark alleyway. Near their gate she paused.

"What are you going to do?"

At once he answered: "Go to Mark Kennicott. Get him out of that jail if I have to fight to do it. And then beg him to do what he can to stop these trail hands from wrecking the town. I was wrong, like I said. Now I will do what I can to straighten things out." He gave her Serringo's gun. "Keep it to protect yourself."

XXIII

George Lockridge, keeping to the deep shadows, made the jail without incident. He paused just outside the door and looked inward. Mark Kennicott was sprawled on the cell cot; the deputy, Wallis, was sunk deeply in a chair fronting the desk. Noiselessly he stepped inside. In two long steps he reached the gun rack and snatched up a shotgun. The noise he made when he cocked the tall rabbit-ear hammers of the weapon brought both Wallis and Kennicott to their feet.

"What the devil . . . ?" Wallis began, staring at the muzzle of the gun.

"Open that cell," Lockridge said.

"What?" Wallis said.

"Let Kennicott out. I've learned a few things this night, and one of them is that he was right. This town needs him, has got to have him. I was one of those responsible for his being locked up. I'm correcting that mistake. Open the cell . . . quick!"

The deputy looked at the twin muzzles of the shotgun.

He moved toward the cell door, picking up the keys as he did so. "You sure have changed, Reverend," he murmured.

"I've had my eyes opened," Lockridge said. He stepped back as Kennicott moved into the room from the small, barred confinement. "Not enough time to tell you the story now, Marshal," he said then to Kennicott. "Let's just say I was wrong. When this is all over with, I'll make my apologies properly."

Kennicott smiled at the tall man. "No apologies necessary. You're not the first one to figure wrong. My thanks for acting when you reached your decision." He paused, swung his attention to the deputy. "Well, Jeff? What's it to be? You with me?"

The deputy hesitated only a moment. He reached to the star pinned to his vest, unfastened it, and handed it to Kennicott. "This is yours, I reckon."

Kennicott accepted it with no comment. He pinned it on, strapped on his gun, and then said: "Maybe mine for just a spell, Jeff. Soon as this fracas is cleared up and the mayor's back, I'll be turning it in. I'm moving on. I'm through here at Cameo Crossing."

"Moving on?"

Kennicott nodded. "I've had my day here. But before I leave, I'll tell the mayor you're the man for the job. Maybe he'll listen to me. You ready?"

The deputy nodded. "Whenever you are, Marshal."

Kennicott turned to the Reverend Lockridge. "It might be a good idea for you to stay off the street. This won't be a pleasant chore. And see that all the women stay inside, too."

Lockridge nodded. "I'll do that." Impulsively he extended his hand. "I'd like to shake your hand, Marshal. And wish you good luck. It was my thick-headedness that put you in this bad position. I'm sorry."

"Forget it," Kennicott said, accepting the minister's hand. "Just keep everybody out of the way. I don't want to see anybody hurt that's not deserving of it."

The minister seemed about to say more but apparently thought better of it. He glanced down at the shotgun in his hands. "Mind if I hang onto this for the night?"

Wallis stared at the tall man's face. "You sure have had a change of mind!" he exclaimed. "I thought you didn't cotton none to such things as guns and shooting?"

"Things happen to change a man's way of thinking," Lockridge said, and wheeled about. "Good luck to you both."

Kennicott watched the minister disappear into the night in thoughtful silence. After a moment he said: "It takes a good man to admit he's wrong." Then he added: "Let's get going."

They moved through the doorway of the jail into the street. The final shadows of the buildings were lying like black, irregularly shaped squares in the dust. Lamps had been lit against the swiftly closing darkness, and, although the day's strong heat at last was broken, the usual evening hush was missing. Now there were wild yells, strident shouts, and gunshots coming from behind the saloon near Crandall's place. And off somewhere beyond the town a dog was barking forlornly.

Wallis laid a hand on Kennicott's arm, halting him. His face serious, the deputy said: "Just in case this don't work out, pardner, I'm saying now I appreciate working with you. And you giving me a second chance after what I pulled this

Ray Hogan

afternoon. Not many would be trusting a man now."

Kennicott said—"Forget it, Jeff."—in a quick sort of way.

"Nope, not apt to," the deputy replied. "You got any special idea in mind about what we're going to do?"

The tall lawman allowed his glance to search slowly along the dark street. "No daylight left," he mused aloud. "And there's not much we can do but hit them one by one. No place around here big enough to serve as a jail for them all. The answer is, of course, to get the top man."

"Overmeyer?"

Kennicott said: "Seringo. He's the key to this. We throw him back in a cell . . . or stop him . . . then we won't have any trouble with the rest."

"You're forgetting McCoy and that drifter, Sprewl."

The lawman shrugged. "One thing at a time. If they show, we'll handle it. Anyway, we don't even know Sprewl's here."

"We just ain't seen him," Wallis observed dourly. "You figure to walk right up and arrest Seringo?"

"It might be the best way, but it could start a wholesale gunfight. I think the thing to do is start out and collect as many guns as we can first. Yank a few stingers and we won't have so many to look out for later on."

They started down the dusty ribbon of gray while the sky beyond grew steadily deeper as the last vestiges of light faded. At their first stop, a rag-tag, run-down saloon owned by a man named Underhill, they entered and found two members of Overmeyer's crew standing at the bar. Seeing Kennicott, Underhill moved quickly from behind his makeshift counter and took up a neutral position out of harm's way in a far corner.

"You OX hands!" Kennicott said. "Turn around easy. With your hands high."

The two cowpunchers came slowly about, a mixture of wonder and surprise on their faces.

152

"You've been warned about wearing guns inside the town."

"We ain't takin' no orders from you," one of the riders replied sullenly.

"Guess again," Kennicott said. "Take their hardware, Jeff."

Wallis moved up to the pair and lifted their weapons from the holsters. Kennicott, his hand resting lightly on the butt of his own pistol, watched them narrowly.

"Stay in here after we leave," he said. "Don't come out on the street unless you want real trouble. You can pick up these guns at the jail when you ride out tomorrow."

"Dave'll take care of you jaspers for this. He warned you about it."

Kennicott grinned at the furious man. "Maybe. But I figure his bark is a lot worse than his bite. Where is he now?"

The two men exchanged glances. "That we wouldn't be knowin'. But never you mind about it. He'll find you, and, when he does, you'll be wishin' you was some place else."

Kennicott said: "Sure, sure. But listen to me good. Stay in here. You follow us out into the street and you might end up dead. Understand?"

Without waiting for a reply he wheeled about and reëntered the street with Wallis at his heels. The deputy paused at the corner of the building and picked up a discarded bushel basket, tossed aside by some housewife. Dropping the two pistols into it, he said: "I'll just tote this along for the rest of the collection. Looks like there might be a right smart of them before we're through."

Kennicott did not reply. His eyes were on the door of Underhill's place. A minute passed and the shadows of the two men appeared in the opening. Kennicott cocked the hammer back of his .45, the sound loud in the momentary hush.

"Step on out, boys," he said. "Let me prove I meant what I said."

The dual shadows vanished at once.

"You think they'll stay in there?" Wallis said.

Kennicott said: "Not for long, but for a little while. Soon as we get out of sight, they'll be legging it for the Trail Queen and Dave Seringo. But this will delay them some."

In the next building, a small café, they found three more OX riders and followed a like procedure with them. To Kennicott's question concerning the whereabouts of Dave Seringo, they also were noncommittal. They did not know. The gunman, Kennicott well knew, could be found inside the Trail Queen. His question was merely for effect, meant to imply he did not know where Dave Seringo was and cared little.

They crossed the street to enter the next structure along the way. It was a bakery and there were no customers within its breathlessly hot walls. But standing there, somewhat back from its one small window, they watched the first two men who had been in Underhill's saloon trot across to the Trail Queen. Seringo would have the news soon.

In the succeeding place they also drew a blank, but in the following one, another small saloon with a card room in the rear, they interrupted a draw poker game long enough to collect four more pistols for Jeff Wallis's basket. After Kennicott and the deputy left, the OX men arose quickly and departed, heading as had the first two for Rohle's.

"Maybe we should've locked them in that room," Wallis said. "That would've kept them out of the way."

"Nothing short of a cell door would hold them after that. Doesn't make much difference now, anyway."

"One good thing, if this keeps on, we'll have them all corralled in the Trail Queen."

Kennicott laughed. "Not such a bad idea, at that."

There were only a few people on the street, now that darkness was offering some degree of protection. Kennicott recognized some of the braver residents, most of whom had some affiliation with Rohle and doubtlessly felt in that was some guarantee of safety. As a whole, the town seemed deserted, however; the majority of those abroad were either OX trail hands or characters of similar stripe who were taking advantage of the opportunity to have themselves a time.

It became apparent shortly after that that Seringo was not the only one apprised of Kennicott's actions in the street. Word was passed quickly along and small groups of OX men began to gather. Kennicott, standing in the deep shadows of a passageway, watched them with thoughtful eyes.

"Looks like collection time is over," he said finally. "Might as well stash that basket somewhere. In there," he added, ducking his head at the alleyway behind them. "We pick up any more, you can just toss them away."

Wallis set the basket down. "It appears to me they might be working up a little reception committee."

Kennicott agreed. "I'll drop back around and circle in on the other side of them," he said. "It'll put me at the other end of the street. They won't be watching that direction. They'll figure we're both down here."

"Good idea," Wallis grunted.

"You stay put here in the dark until you see me. Watch that spot of light there in front of Kane's place. When you see me walk into that, you come out and start down to meet me. I'll do the rest. Understand?"

Wallis said: "Yes, I understand."

Kennicott turned to leave, to double back through the narrow passage lying between the two buildings in front of which they presently stood. He took one step and paused.

"Jeff?"

"Yeah."

"Mind what I said. Don't move out of here until you see me.

155

I don't want you out there alone. Anybody comes along, let them go."

Through the inky darkness Wallis said: "All right, Marshal."

Kennicott moved off along the corridor, stepping over the basket of guns taken from OX riders, stumbling a little against the accumulated trash whipped into the narrow space by the winds. He reached the end and turned left, planning to swing wide of the buildings and come back to the street, as he had explained to Wallis, at a point near Leo Kane's livery stable. Closing in on the riders with drawn guns, from both sides, as they would then be doing, should turn the trick. At least it was worth a gamble.

XXIV

Left alone in the darkness at the end of the passageway, Jeff Wallis listened idly to Kennicott's retreating footsteps. He kept his glance down the street, however, to the groups of men forming along the way at various intervals. This was going to be a night the town would long remember, one that would go down in the books in blood red, he was sure.

He was glad Kennicott was back on the job as marshal. Being honest with himself, he doubted if he would have been able to cope alone with such a critical emergency as was shaping up, had they called upon him to do so. A man like Kennicott could. There was something cool and deadly about the big lawman that was reassuring, that gave you confidence and a feeling of security when he was on the job. And, conversely, instilled an inclination on the part of the lawless to tread softly in his presence. He had been a fool to think he could measure up and wear a marshal's star and make it mean something. Some are cut out to be a ramrod, a leader, as was Kennicott; others, like himself, were meant to follow along and take orders.

But it was a mighty fine feeling having one dream in a lifetime come true, even if for only a few brief hours, even if under circumstances that were not flattering. He had studied about it all afternoon, wondering if he should ignore the warning Dave Seringo had flung at him and forget the orders Rohle had issued and be his own man, go out in the street and do his job as he knew it should be done, regardless of them. But he had not and that disturbed him. Whether it was due to the endless years of experience at taking orders, of being a follower and never leader, or if it was that he was simply afraid, he actually did not know.

In reality his bravery had never been tested or tried. Always, in time of danger, he had been with Mark Kennicott and had simply done as he was told. Just as he was doing now, waiting there in the shadows out of harm's way until the marshal appeared at the far end of the street. And it took no particular courage to perform that task.

Later, when he would start down the street, there would be little danger for him. Kennicott would have drawn the attention of the waiting men to himself. If there was to be gun play, it would be by Kennicott. He would serve only as a rear guard, a threat and discouragement, and would likely see no action of any sort.

In a vague sort of way it angered Jeff Wallis. He never got a chance to learn if he possessed the necessary skills and courage to accomplish a thing of value. Kennicott always kept him out of the line of fire, pushed him into the background if the situation got bad. For his own satisfaction he would really like to know if he could stand and deliver if the time ever came when it was necessary.

The sound of iron tires grating against the sand reached him then and, turning, he saw Callie Heaston's buggy enter the end of the street and head for Jergenson's. Coming in to pick up her daughter. He watched her draw abreast, debating with himself if he should warn her to be careful or remain quiet as Kennicott had ordered him. The widow had been a part of his plans for the future, too, but she had not known it. Now she never would. He let her pass without drawing her attention, hearing faintly but not distinguishing the chatter of the twins in the rear seat of the worn, old vehicle.

There was a sudden commotion at the front of the Trail Queen. The doors flung wide and a man, propelled by another grasping him by collar and seat, came rushing awkwardly into the open and sprawled full length in the dust. Wallis studied the man, now getting up slowly and dusting at his baggy overalls. It was old Pete, a stable roustabout. Getting thrown out of saloons was no new experience to him. Wallis watched the cowboy, apparently an OX rider who had done the heaving, swagger back into the Trail Queen.

He stepped aside just as he reached the batwings. Two more men came out and halted on the porch. One was Clete McCoy, the other was an Overmeyer man who had helped disarm Kennicott earlier in the day. They conversed for a long minute, now and then glancing down the street in the general direction of where Wallis stood.

That they knew he was there and that their conversation pertained to him was evident. After a time they separated, McCoy swinging off the porch and beyond the fan of yellow light coming through the saloon doorway and disappearing into the blackness alongside the building. The OX rider sauntered into the street and began leisurely to make his way toward the deputy.

Wallis eyed him sharply, some deep, inner warning sounding its alarm. He allowed the man to drift closer, at the same time trying to search out from the enveloping blackness across the way the figure of Clete McCoy. The scar-faced man was there somewhere. When the OX rider was no more than twenty feet distant, he drew his gun.

"Hold it right there, mister!"

The man eased to a halt. "That you, Marshal?" he asked cautiously.

"I'm Wallis. The deputy."

"Where's the marshal? Hear he's pluckin' iron along the street. Thought maybe he'd like to make a try for mine."

"He's around. And if you're wearing a gun, better drop it where you stand. They's a law against wearing one inside the town limits."

"So I heard before."

"Then, walk up here closer with your hands up," Wallis said. He was going against Kennicott's instructions but there seemed to be no choice. Anyway, if this man was gunning for the marshal, this would be a good chance to put him out of the action for a few minutes, at least. "I'll take that iron. You get it back when you leave town."

The OX cowpuncher raised his arms slowly, indolently. "Reckon you know you're in a powerful lot of trouble, Deputy. Seringo told you to keep the marshal locked up. You didn't do what he said and Dave's sure not going to like it."

"To hell with Dave," Wallis said. He was on his own at last. Mark Kennicott was not standing by to back him up or to tell him what to do. His legs were trembling a bit, but from excitement, not fear.

"Keep your hands high," he said.

He threw a long glance down the street toward Kane's.

Kennicott was still not to be seen. However, he would have to get this little affair handled quickly for the marshal was about due. He couldn't be involved when Mark started his play.

"Come on, come on," he said. "Start backing toward me. Ain't got the whole blame' night."

From across the street, from the dark mouth of the opposing passageway lying between two buildings, Clete McCoy said:

Ray Hogan

"What's the hurry, Jeff? You ain't goin' no place."

Wallis was immediately aware that he was in a bad position, caught at one point of a triangle formed by the three of them. McCoy evidently had dropped back behind the structures across the way and moved to a place where he had a clear view. Without shifting his gun from the OX cowpuncher, he said coolly: "What's on your mind, Clete?"

"The marshal," McCoy said, "but you'll do for a starter." He fired.

Wallis saw the bloom of the gun and felt the shocking impact of the bullet in the self-same fragment of time. He staggered back, somewhat astonished that he was unable to control his legs. His pistol dropped from his hand and he cursed himself for his awkwardness, not realizing he had no strength left with which to hold it. McCoy's gun shattered the night again. Once more he jolted under the thundering blow. It hurled him back, deeper into the passageway. Something caught at his faltering heels. He fell, sprawling, one arm draping across the basket of guns he had earlier hidden there.

Dimly, at the end of the narrow corridor, he could make out McCoy's looming shape: a vague shadow poised insolently against the faint spray of light from lamplit windows. He heard the scar-faced gunman's mocking laughter.

"One of those bullets was for your friend the marshal. But you got them both. I got plenty left for him. I'm hopin' you enjoy them."

Wallis's twitching fingers felt the cold steel of a gun barrel in the basket. It was an effort to grasp it, to lift it and lay it across the rim of the wicker and aim it at McCoy's outline. It took every remaining ounce of strength within him to pull back the hammer and squeeze off the trigger.

But there was enough consciousness left for him to see Mc-Coy slam sideways and spin half around as the slug ripped into his chest. Through glazing eyes he watched McCoy buckle at the knees and sink, breath rattling in his throat.

"And I . . . got a bullet for you," Wallis muttered just as complete blackness closed in on him.

XXV

Kennicott, moving silently as a cat, halted at the edge of the alley, a block north of where he had stationed Jeff Wallis. Before him lay a narrow street and he laid his sharp, probing glance along its every foot.

Suddenly a gunshot rocked the darkness. He wheeled swiftly about. It seemed to have come from the passageway where the deputy was waiting. Another blast echoed. And then a third. He waited no longer. The shots had come from the corridor, without a doubt. Wallis was in trouble.

A premonition clutching at him and less cautious than usual, Kennicott circled the building at a fast trot and came boldly into the street. He halted beside a roof support and threw his glance ahead.

A body lay at the edge of the walk, half on, half off. Several men had already gathered and now were talking in low voices. Two more were coming at a run from the Trail Queen, attracted not by the gunshots that were common enough that night but by the assemblage. Kennicott's throat tightened. Death was no stranger to him, of course, but the knowledge that it could be Jeff Wallis lying there gripped him with an odd, angry feeling of loss. He could not make out the body distinctly. Was it Jeff or someone else?

One of the onlookers answered his questions. "The deputy was standin' back there in the dark. He was talkin' to Beaver when this McCoy feller started shootin' from across the street. Reckon he figured he'd done him up good 'cause he walked over and was just standin' here, gabbin' when the deputy nailed him."

"Both dead?"

"Yep, deader'n staked crows. Two bullets in the deputy, one in McCoy. Sure must have took a lot of sand for that deputy to shoot back. Bet he was 'most clear dead by that time."

An unreasoning fury rocked Kennicott. He shoved his way forward, roughly shouldering a path through the half circle of men. One of them, knocked off balance, lashed out with the back of his hand.

"Dammit! Watch what you're doing!"

Kennicott struck him alongside the head with the barrel of his gun, knocking him flat to the street. He did not hesitate or look back but moved on until he was kneeling beside the fallen deputy. He struck a match with a thumbnail and hopefully examined Wallis. Both bullets were in the chest. He lay on his back, one arm hanging loosely across the basket of OX guns. He was dead.

"That you back there, Mark?" Cartwright's voice reached in to him from the end of the corridor.

"It's me, Doc. Jeff's here. Dead."

The physician started along the passageway, picking his steps over the trash, muttering: "All this danged shooting. I knew somebody was going to get killed."

Kennicott had risen. "They ganged up on him," he said in a low voice. "It wasn't any accident. McCoy, and one of the OX crowd. Broached him from two points, likely. Either they were looking for me and ran into him instead, or they set out to get rid of him so I'd have nobody to side me. Well, he fooled them a bit. He took care of Clete for me. Now it's my turn to handle the rest."

The little doctor seemed not to hear. Over his shoulder he called to the street: "Couple of you men come get this body.

Take it and the other over to my place. My wife will show you where to put 'em." He turned to face Kennicott. "Your turn to do what?"

"Handle Seringo and the rest of King Overmeyer's bunch. If I don't do it now, there'll be more dead men by sunup."

Cartwright said: "You're talking like an idiot. You can't do that alone. Try it and you'll be one of those dead men you're worrying about."

"I haven't got much choice. This killing will set things off for sure, and, if I don't step in now, the OX crowd will figure this town is theirs and really start taking it over."

"I still say you can't do it alone, and you won't have any backing from the good citizens."

Kennicott made no immediate reply. He walked slowly back to the street, the doctor at his heels. He paused there and threw his glance along the building fronts, his face looking stretched, all hard planes and sharp angles, and his eyes were deep, fathomless pockets. Cameo Crossing seemed strangely deserted.

"They're guessing you'll try just what you've been talking about," Cartwright said. "Right now they're all just waiting for you inside Rohle's place. You're a fool to go in there, Mark. Your job doesn't call for you standing up against two dozen or more gun-happy trail hands."

"Only one. Maybe two," Kennicott said in a thoughtful way. "Seringo's the man to stop. Overmeyer, maybe, but I figure it's Seringo. Get him out of the picture and we'll have no trouble with the rest."

"You won't be dealing with him alone," Cartwright warned. "They'll gang up on you sure."

Kennicott shook his head. "I know Seringo's kind. They're all alike. They think first of their reputation, and they'll have no help from no man. They want the glory for themselves."

"I'm not thinking about that. I'm thinking about what happens afterward if you down Seringo. What makes you think you won't have to buck all the rest of them? Seringo's their fair-haired boy and they won't take kindly to having him dropped."

"Like I said, I have to take my chances," Kennicott answered, brushing the fact aside. "Now, I'd like to ask a favor of you. You and the reverend are to see what you can do to keep everybody off the street. If things go wrong, that OX bunch will do some mighty big celebrating."

Cartwright studied the lawman's expressionless features in the feeble light from a nearby window for a moment. Then: "All right, Mark, if this is the way you want it. We'll get the word out to stay off the street. Though I don't see much need for it," he added, turning his eyes along the walk. Suddenly he held out his stubby-fingered hand. "Good luck," he said then, and hurried off.

Kennicott ducked his head at the retreating shape of the physician and watched him make his way toward the Lockridge place. He waited until he saw him turn into the parsonage yard, and then swung his attention back to the Trail Queen. The place was abnormally quiet for that time of night, the subdued murmur of low voices being the only sound emanating from the bulking structure. They expected him; they were waiting for him.

He grinned wryly into the darkness. He wouldn't disappoint them, but he would arrive on his own terms—through the back and not the front as they likely expected him to do. He started along the row of silent buildings, the hollow rap of his boot heels seeming unusually loud in the night. He reached the corner opposite Jergenson's Café and halted, again allowing his eyes to prowl the empty street. A buggy stood at Jergenson's rail, and he started, recognizing it as Callie Heaston's. She had come for Alberta, of course, but she had not left. What was she doing there? In town that night was the last place he wanted her and her daughters. He left the boardwalk and headed across the street. He would see them aboard and to the edge of town. Then he would return to the business at hand.

"Mark! It's Sprewl . . . look out!"

It was Alberta's frantic voice. It reached him just as he came into the dead center of the street. He lunged to one side instinctively, catching a stir of movement just beyond the buggy. But he was uncertain—it could be Alberta. He delayed, for the briefest instant, the pressure of his finger upon the trigger.

A gun flamed bright orange in the blackness. The hushed buildings rocked with the echo as he felt the bullet burn against his ribs. He threw himself to the street, firing as he did so, not at the movement he had seen that apparently had been Alberta, but at a point near the rear corner of Jergenson's building. Sprewl's gun blasted again and dust spurted inches from his face. But it gave him his target. He answered quickly, two closely spaced shots. Sprewl yelled and stumbled out into the open yard. He staggered against a pile of empty boxes, kindling for Jergenson's cook stove, recoiled, and fell heavily. For a long minute Kennicott watched him from his prone position in the street, and, when there was no sign of life, he arose and walked to the gunman's side.

Alberta and Callie Heaston came out of the dark and crowded up to him, asking questions, half crying. Kennicott brushed them aside. He rolled Sprewl to his back, assuring himself the man was dead.

He looked down at the girl. "Thanks for the warning. I wasn't expecting him."

"He's been hiding out here, waiting for you," she answered. "I was afraid I wouldn't yell in time." Kennicott glanced toward the Trail Queen. A half dozen men, attracted by the gunshots, stood on the porch in front of the doors. None had come into the street. "Where are the twins?" he asked then of Callie.

"Inside. With the Jergensons."

"Get them and drive down to the parson's. You'll be safer there in case anything starts."

"If anything starts . . . ," Callie began falteringly.

"Hurry," Kennicott pressed gently. He had opened the loading gate of his pistol and was replacing the spent cartridges. "I'm going to finish this thing up now."

XXVI

He waited there beside Jergenson's place until Callie Heaston and her daughters were in the buggy and moving off down the street. Not until he saw the vehicle, dim and indistinct in the night, pull up before the parsonage did he return his attention to the business at hand.

He was thinking many thoughts in those fleeting moments; the days, the hours, and the months he had spent in Cameo Crossing, the friends he had made there. Even the buildings were like old acquaintances. And perhaps he was seeing them for the last time.

But he would have to do what must be done. What he planned was not a smart thing, considered by the odds, but he must carry out his responsibilities in hope it would prove the best for the town. If he could put Seringo out of the way, maybe those who would destroy Cameo Crossing and turn it into a prostituted haven for outlaws and uncontrolled violence would move on. If they didn't and he managed to stay alive through the night, it would be up to the town then. He would do his part, what his conscience told him was expected of him, but when that was finished, he could do no more. It would be their problem and maybe—just maybe—the townspeople would awake and realize the true issue. And then act.

He swung his glance to the jail. A light was shining through the window. It made him think of George Lockridge, the man who hated guns and killing but who now knew the truth. He was happy the minister had come to a realization, that he finally understood his ideas were good but far ahead of their time in places such as Cameo Crossing. Someday it would be the way Lockridge wanted it, law and order administered in a peaceable manner. It was years in the future but it was good to know Lockridge accepted the situation for he could be of great help to the town.

He started then for the Trail Queen, his thinking done, his remembering over with. The job was at hand. He walked in slow, deliberate strides, his shadow reaching out behind him, making him a man ten foot tall with monstrous shoulders and arms. The three or four men who had been loitering near the batwing doors of the saloon wheeled swiftly and suddenly disappeared.

He glanced upward, to the window that marked Walker Rohle's second-story quarters. The shades were not drawn and a lamp, set back deep in the rooms, had been lit. But if Rohle were watching, he was standing off to one side and not visible from the street. In the final analysis of the situation, the struggle lay between Rohle and himself, Kennicott knew. When this night was over, one or the other would have won the town.

"This is what you wanted, Walker," he murmured.

He reached the Trail Queen's porch and mounted. Again his glance swept the forlorn, abandoned strip of dust with its twin lines of empty, dark-eyed buildings. There was nothing; no one to be seen. He was utterly alone. There was only himself and Dave Seringo and all those who backed the gunman awaiting him within the saloon.

He crossed the gallery in slow, measured steps and paused just outside the doors. He stood there, allowing the light to strike his eyes and waited for his vision to change and become accustomed to the glare. Inside, noise had dwindled to a mere murmur—hoarse whispers, the muted clink of glass against glass, the smothered laugh of a woman. Above the batwings he could see the coils of smoke hanging along the ceiling, circling gently around the lamps. The strong, rank smell of stale beer and spilled whiskey and sweaty, unwashed bodies was like a suffocating cloud.

Satisfied his eyes had reverted to normal ability, he pushed the doors inward and stepped quickly within, moving a few steps away from the entrance as a protective measure. He was ready for instant action, not knowing if Seringo would greet him with a blazing gun. There was only a dead silence, a complete hush through which tension suddenly built into a tangible, nerve-crushing pressure.

Seringo was facing him. He stood near center of a half circle of OX men, a step and a half in front of them. He was without coat and his crimson red sleeve garters hitched up his cuffs to a point well above his wrists. His hat was on the back of his head and the single, well-worn, bone-handled gun he carried hung low on his right thigh. With his feet spread apart, braced, he gave Kennicott the impression of a tightly coiled spring awaiting only the touch of a finger to unleash and strike.

Kennicott met his empty, slate blue eyes and the expectant glances of the OX crew with level gaze. He was the law; he was authority and they knew it. And that was good. It put them at a slight disadvantage—one lone lawman daring to brace them all. It turned them vaguely uneasy, uncertain. Which was the way it should be. The power and the prestige of the law should work that way, fearless, facing any and all odds. In that moment Mark Kennicott was all the lawmen of the frontier facing up unafraid to all the gunmen and outlaws and hardcases who ever rode the Owlhoot Trail.

In a voice that reached every corner of the saloon he said: "Seringo! You're under arrest!"

The gunman eyed him with an amused smirk. He swept the men standing behind him with a sidelong glance.

"You know the answer to that one, Marshal."

Kennicott nodded. "I expect I do. You'd have it no other way. But you're a fool, Dave. It's not necessary. Getting killed over a little thing like wearing a gun when the town's ordinance says you can't is a sucker deal."

Seringo laughed, a dry, mirthless sound. "The way you talk, a man would think this is all cut and dried. That I'm already a-layin' out there on Boot Hill."

"You the same as are, Dave, if you go through with this. I know you . . . and I know what I can do. You're a dead man if you try to draw on me."

There was the faintest lift of surprise in the gunman's expression. He glared at the lawman. Overmeyer, somewhat drunk, pushed through the circle of men.

"He's only tryin' to bluff you, Dave! Don't be listenin' to his palaver. When this shootin's over, we'll be totin' him to Boot Hill, not you."

Kennicott shrugged. "Your friend talks a good fight, when you're doing the fighting," he said. "Why don't you let him stand for you, Dave?"

Suddenly angry Overmeyer said: "An' if you do get lucky and beat Dave, what makes you think you'll walk out of here? I got twenty men here that'll see you don't!" The Texan wheeled about. "You hear me, boys? If Dave goes down, you take care of this lawman! Understand?"

There was a mutter through the crowd. Seringo shook his head.

"Don't get in such a hurry. I ain't dead yet," he said. But his voice was not quite so certain, his expression a trifle less positive.

Kennicott, his eyes never once leaving the gunman, said to

Overmeyer: "If that's the way you want it, King, that's how we'll play it. But I'll have four, maybe five bullets left in this gun and one of them will be for you. Figure on that."

He heard then the faintest drag of sound behind him. He tensed, wondering if he had been wrong, if more OX men were sliding in behind him. His eyes, fastened to Seringo and seeing also the riders directly behind the gunman, saw a change of expression come into their faces.

In the next moment he heard the familiar voice of George Lockridge say: "Just to keep this a fair fight, we figured to drop by."

From the tail of his vision he saw the tall minister drift in upon his left shoulder. There were others, too—Leo Kane, a shotgun in his big hands, paused on his right. And behind them were Doc Cartwright with a long-barreled cap and ball .44 ready for use, John Quincy the baker, Burt Carmer the barber, and several more including Callie Heaston, also armed, Judith and Alberta. And Tom Girard.

An odd feeling traveled through Kennicott. They had come to back his play, letting him know he was no longer alone. They stood no chance against men like Overmeyer and his crew, but it didn't matter; they were willing to take their chances right along with him in defense of their town. A strong pride swept through Kennicott; a man could buck a lot of tall odds for people like those.

But he could not allow them to get hurt. Over his shoulder he said: "I appreciate this, folks, but it's no place for you. This is my fight."

Girard said: "Ours, too, Mark. It took us a spell to arrive at that way of looking at it, but we know it now. We don't aim to take a hand unless we have to. We're just here to keep it even."

The effect upon the OX riders was plain. Where they had been belligerent and expectant, jackals awaiting a kill feast, they now turned restless and uneasy. Overmeyer frowned darkly and rubbed at his chin. Only Seringo was untouched by it all. He watched Kennicott with a dull, steady hatred, completely unaware, it seemed, of the altering force.

Kennicott moved a few steps to his left, getting from in front of the townspeople. "You coming along, Seringo? Or do we do it the hard way?"

Nothing about the gunman changed. Nothing save the slight twitching of his colorless lips. In the breathless hush he murmured: "No. Not now, not ever."

He broke for his gun at that point. His hand flashed down and came up in a single, fluid blur. Two guns shattered the stillness of the big room. Black smoke belched upward and began to drift lazily about the overhead lamps. Kennicott felt the tug at his shoulder but ignored it. He crouched for a second shot. His eyes were on the straining figure of Dave Seringo, indistinct and weaving slightly in the cordite haze.

Through the thinning smoke he saw then it would not be necessary to shoot twice. The gunman, his cornered face surprised, stared at him over the distance. Sheer reflex drew him to his toes, caused him to try and lift the gun in his stiffening fingers. He had no strength. The weapon slipped from his fingers and fell to the floor. He toppled heavily upon it.

"Don't any of you move!" Callie Heaston's voice suddenly charged through the silence. "Not unless you want both barrels of this buckshot straight in your middles!"

Kennicott, surprised, half turned to look at the woman. This was a different Callie, a new Callie he had not known—one who, at last, had accepted the West and was taking her place in it.

"Mark! Upstairs!"

Judith's shrill warning struck through the pall of smoke. Kennicott wheeled and threw his glance to the balcony. Walker

Rohle was standing there with a Derringer in his hand. But the man's eyes were on King Overmeyer.

"I'm backing the marshal, too," Rohle said in an odd, high-pitched voice. "I'll shoot if anyone makes a wrong move!"

There was a long moment of stunned silence, and then Tom Girard spoke. "Little late to be changin' horses, Walker," he said dryly.

Someone laughed, and in that single, small sound of mockery and ridicule Walker Rohle was destroyed forever and all time in Cameo Crossing. His face flushed and his shoulders went down. The arm holding the Derringer dropped to his side. Without another word he wheeled and entered his office, closing the door behind him softly.

Kennicott drew a deep breath. He turned his attention to Overmeyer. That was yet to be finished. "What about it, King?"

The Texan met his gaze momentarily, and then looked away. "I reckon we'll be ridin', Marshal," he said, and started for the doorway. Quietly his crew fell in behind him.

"One thing more," Kennicott called after him, "this town stays closed to you! Don't try again."

Overmeyer made no reply but passed on through the batwing doors into the night's darkness.

Jeff Wallis was dead. Clete McCoy and the flat-eyed gunman, Dave Seringo, also lay beneath the earth on Boot Hill. But Cameo Crossing still lived.

Walker Rohle had departed during the night, making arrangements with Paris Humboldt, the banker, to dispose of his holdings and forward the proceeds to an address he would later supply. Kennicott stood on the porch of the parsonage and watched the town going about its normal business and everyday living routine.

"It's a peaceful place, after yesterday . . . and last night," he said, turning to Judith.

She pressed his arm. "Maybe it will stay that way now, Mark."

He shook his head. "There's always the Rohles . . . the Seringos and the Overmeyers in one shape or another. I doubt if the world will ever run out of them."

"Perhaps, but my guess is they will steer wide of Cameo Crossing for a long time."

"I hope so," he said. He took her by the shoulders with his broad hands. "We've had no chance to talk about us since all this started. If it's not too late, I'm ready now to move on. To go ahead with the plans we had in mind when the trouble began."

Judith returned his gaze. Only three days since they had talked of it, it seemed so much longer. She studied his sober face, reading his thoughts.

Smiling a little she said: "Why should we leave Cameo Crossing now? It's a good town. Safe and quiet and a fine place to raise a family. Besides," she added, "you'll be needing this marshal's job to support a family."

Kennicott gaped at her, for the instant set back by her words. A grin broke across his wind-tanned face. Without a word he drew her close and kissed her fully on the lips. It was a wonderful feeling that possessed him, the knowledge that she understood, that she, too, recognized his responsibilities and was willing to share them from that moment on.

No man could ask for more.

ABOUT THE AUTHOR

Ray Hogan was an author who inspired a loyal following over the years since he published his first Western novel, *Ex-Marshal,* in 1956. Hogan was born in Willow Springs, Missouri, where his father was town marshal. At five the Hogan family moved to Albuquerque where they lived in the foothills of the Sandia and Manzano Mountains. His father was on the Albuquerque police force and, in later years, owned the Overland Hotel. It was while listening to his father and other old-timers tell tales from the past that Ray was inspired to recast these tales in fiction. From the beginning he did exhaustive research into the history and the people of the Old West, and the walls of his study were lined with various firearms, spurs, pictures, books, and memorabilia, about all of which he could talk in dramatic detail. "I've attempted to capture the courage and bravery of those men and women that lived out West and the dangers and problems they had to overcome," Hogan once remarked. If his lawmen protagonists seem sometimes larger than life, it is because they are men of integrity, heroes who through grit of character and common sense are able to overcome the obstacles they encounter despite often overwhelming odds. This same grit of character can also be found in Hogan's heroines, and in *The Vengeance of Fortuna West* (1983) Hogan wrote a gripping and totally believable account of a woman who takes up the badge and tracks the men who killed her lawman husband by ambush. No less intriguing in her way is Nellie Dupray, convicted of rustling in *The Glory Trail* (1978). One of his most popular books, dealing with an earlier period in the West with Kit Carson as its protagonist, is *Soldier in Buckskin* (Five Star Westerns, 1996). Above all, what is most impressive about Hogan's Western novels is the consistent quality with which each is crafted, the compelling depth of his characters, and his ability to juxtapose the complexities of human conflict into narratives always as intensely interesting as they are emotionally involving. *Law Comes to Lawless* will be his next Five Star Western.